BLOOD LINE

BLOOD LINE

An Inspector Faro Novel

Alanna Knight

St. Martin's Press
New York

BLOODLINE: AN INSPECTOR FARO MYSTERY. Copyright © 1989 by Alanna Knight. All
rights reserved. Printed in the United States of America. No part of this book
may be used or reproduced in any manner whatsoever without written
permission except in the case of brief quotations embodied in critical articles or
reviews. For information, address St. Martin's Press, 175 Fifth Avenue, New
York, N.Y. 10010.

Library of Congress Cataloging-in-Publication Data

Knight, Alanna.
        Blood line : an Inspector Faro mystery / Alanna Knight.
            p.   cm.
        "A Thomas Dunne book."
        ISBN 0-312-03295-1
        I. Title.
    PR6061.N45B55   1989
    823'.914—dc20   89-30425
                                                                         CIP

First published in Great Britain by Macmillan London Limited.

First U.S. Edition

10 9 8 7 6 5 4 3 2 1

for
Patricia and Kevin

Chapter One

When the body was found Detective Inspector Jeremy Faro was at home at 9 Sheridan Place, taking afternoon tea with his mother and two small daughters, Rose and Emily. Basking in the rare and somewhat ill-fitting role of father, he hoped that the recent decrease in crime would continue, encouraged perhaps by an August unusually hot for Edinburgh. It would indeed be a pleasant change if he, in common with the City Police and Sheriff Court, might enjoy the small miracle of a respite from vice and law breaking.

He was to be disappointed.

Earlier that month, his mother had written from Orkney advising him to expect her on the 'long-promised' holiday in his new house. After careful deliberation and much heart searching, she had decided to brave the voyage to the mainland.

'We must put our trust in the Lord', she wrote, 'that this horrid Prussian war will not spread to our dear land. I tremble at the thought of victorious French troops marching along Princes Street.'

Jeremy Faro had long since decided that his mother's morbid interest in wars and rebellions was worthy of the Queen herself, whose lengthy retreats to her beloved Balmoral much perturbed her Parliament and angered Prime Minister Gladstone.

Personally, Faro was more concerned with the chaos to be expected from this imminent domestic invasion, and, guilt-ridden by his own neglect of the duties of fatherhood, he lay awake composing particularly convincing letters to his determined parent. In the cold light of day the excuse that his house was not yet in order sounded feeble indeed. The truth was less palatable. 1870 had been notable for a tide of personal misfortunes: suspected typhoid, followed by a disastrous love affair, its wounds still too fresh and raw to leave him emotionally capable of dealing with his two exuberant children who, he had sadly to admit, were in danger of becoming strangers to him.

Needless to say, the letters remained unwritten in his head. Every inch the devoted parent, he awaited the Orkney boat at Leith and, with great tenderness, received his two small daughters into his arms.

Mrs Brook, housekeeper at Sheridan Place, regarded the scene with considerable satisfaction. A simple woman, she firmly believed that every man should have his mate. Not for his own amusement had the Almighty ordained that the animals should enter the ark two by two. In her below stairs stronghold, Mrs Brook nodded approvingly as the normally sober household of Inspector Faro and his stepson, Dr Vincent Beaumarcher Laurie, echoed to girlish squeals of delight.

'Come – see this – and this.' Rose and Emily, accustomed to the flat treeless landscapes of their Orkney home, exclaimed wide-eyed as Edinburgh's extinct volcano, Arthur's Seat, filled the horizon from the drawing-room window, while the dining room offered an undulating, sun-shimmering vista of the Pentland Hills. There was even a ginger kitten called Rusty, who had escaped from the kitchen to see what all the fuss was about.

The appearance of their stepbrother, alighting from a gig, brought a fresh wave of excitement. Especially as Vince, who never neglected to bring them gifts, unleashed an armful of picture books and paint-boxes.

Mrs Brook, beaming, delivered her *coup de grâce*. An afternoon tea, calculated to win the hearts of two girls and the secret envy of their grandmother. Pancakes, feather light, with jam made from the garden's strawberries, a Dundee cake stuffed with fruit and enticing small iced cakes.

Looking over the scene Faro felt unusually paternal, the bachelor quarters suddenly transformed into the home they might have been had he remarried, as his mother had sincerely hoped he would after Lizzie's death. Wistfully he thought of the difference that female presences brought with them and how this sometimes sterile dining room was now a place warm and glowing, echoing to the affection of these eager young people.

There were undoubted changes since his last meeting with his two daughters. After an absence of some months, he saw in six-year-old Emily for the first time an extraordinary resemblance to Vince, Lizzie's illegitimate son.

'Yes, of course I'll take you to Arthur's Seat.'

'And the Castle, please, dear Vince,' said Emily. Wonders were not over. The animated expressions of the two, their fair curls, brought to life his dear dead Lizzie as she had looked long ago.

'I want to go to Holyrood Palace, Vince. I want to see where Queen Mary lived. After all she was a Stuart too – like us,' said Rose, who would soon be nine. Her dark prettiness and delicate features were inherited from his diminutive mother, who had been a Sinclair Stuart before she married Police Constable Magnus Faro.

Vince and Jeremy exchanged wry glances over the girls' heads. Obviously Mary Faro had been at work filling those same small heads with romantic nonsense. All Sinclairs and Stuarts on the islands claimed descent from Queen Mary's half-brother the wicked Lord Robert, Earl of Orkney, who had tyrannised the islands and whose sons, legitimate and bastard, notorious for rape and seduction, were largely responsible for increasing the population with their innumerable offspring.

'At least Queen Mary couldn't claim a seal woman for a great-grandmother,' murmured Vince.

The girls' grandmother overheard his remark and said acidly, 'It happens to be true, young man, so do not give me your learned doctor's talk on the subject. I know what I'm talking about. I lived with her and she was a very, very odd lady. She even had webbed toes and her long black hair was just like a seal's coat. Why, I remember . . . '

Jeremy Faro finished his tea and retired to the sofa. There he sat back contentedly, happy to remain a spectator in a good-natured argument. Rose and Emily speedily followed his example. With four soft arms around his neck and two soft, sweet faces staring up into his, and a small plump hand occasionally reaching up to stroke his face or kiss his cheek, he was content. There was healing grace as well as pride in the almost forgotten rituals of fatherhood.

At that moment Mrs Brook entered with a constable at her heels.

Taking in the scene, he said, 'May I have a word, sir?'

Trouble, thought Faro. Dammit.

Out of earshot in the corridor, the constable said, 'There's been an accident, man's body found near the foot of Castle Rock.' Hearing the laughter and excited children's voices issuing from behind the closed door, he said, 'Sorry to disturb you like this, Inspector. We were all for moving the corpse straight to the mortuary, but we've been warned by Superintendent Mackintosh that you and Doctor Laurie, as the Police Surgeon's assistant, are to have a look first. Is that right, sir?'

'It is indeed, Constable.'

Returning momentarily to the dining room and consoling his family with a murmured, 'Something we have to look into. We'll be back soon,' he summoned Vince and boarded the waiting police carriage, which bounded across the Meadows and along Johnston Terrace past the King's Stables Road.

Climbing over the railings and up the steep slope to where the two constables stood on guard, Faro and Vince looked down at the twisted broken body under the rough blanket. The sight outraged Faro's senses. Used as he was to sudden death, the contrast between the world of childhood's innocence and family life he had just left, and the cold clay that had once been a dignified elderly man,

10

that dark unholy violence lurking within a summer's day, seemed obscene in its sudden transition.

'Nothing has been touched, Constable?'

'Nothing, sir. Just as we found him after he was spotted from the battlements. One of the Castle guards. Thought it was an old sack.'

Darkness overtook the sun, a clap of thunder followed by a sudden heavy shower. Above them the Castle shimmered through a rain shroud, wrapped in ancient sinister majesty.

Vince followed his stepfather's upward gaze. 'If I am not mistaken, those are the windows of Queen Mary's apartments.'

'Aye, lad. And what a treasure trove for any thief.'

The constable hovered. 'Sure you don't want the corpse taken in, sir? You'd be a lot more comfortable in the mortuary.'

At Faro's sharp refusal, the man's expression as he buttoned up his cape clearly indicated that he thought his superior officer was mad. And it was no secret that Superintendent Mackintosh thought so too: that it was carrying things too far for everything to be left precisely as it was whenever they found a corpse where no corpse should rightly be. If there was a mystery to be investigated and maybe a murder to be solved then they were to wait for Inspector Faro.

Most of the constables agreed that it was very high-handed behaviour, but the Inspector had been adamant. There were too many cases of vital clues being lost for ever, he pointed out, when a body was removed to the mortuary before on-the-spot examination.

Faro knew of one case personally where a policeman had even tidied up a bedroom in the New Town when a woman was brutally murdered, so that her modesty would not be outraged by appearing naked. By the time Faro reached the scene all evidence had disappeared. Evidence, he was certain, that would incriminate her jealous husband as her murderer and not her lover who, protesting his innocence, was found guilty.

Helpless to prove his theory, after that incident, as senior detective he reserved the right, unpleasant as it was, to first view all victims at the scene of the crime.

'How did it happen?'

'He must have been trying to break into the royal apartments – there's a window right above us. Up to no good, Inspector, mark my words.'

Vince stood up from his brief examination. 'Rigor has set in a long while past. He must have been here for some time, concealed from the road by this ridge and the hours of darkness.'

'It also rained quite heavily last night, just like this, I suspect,' said Faro, gloomily turning up his greatcoat collar. With a last searching glance at the great bulk of the Castle, which continued to stare down malevolently through the rain sheets, he and Vince turned the body over, trying as they did so to disturb as little as possible, in that first vital search for clues.

'Take particular notice of his garments, Vince. Do they suggest anything to you?'

Vince shook his head and his stepfather continued. 'Here is additional proof of his lying on this very spot for some considerable time. Feel how wet the back of his jacket is, and yet underneath where he lay, face downwards, his shirt and the front of his breeches are quite dry, as is the ground beneath him. Interesting.'

There was no means of identification forthcoming. The man's pockets were empty and leaving the constables in charge of a somewhat cursory routine search, Faro and Vince once more boarded the police carriage, with the corpse on a stretcher in the back.

By the time they had arrived at the Central Office of the Edinburgh City Police, Faro, who remained silent throughout the short journey, had already reached several significant conclusions.

'I doubt whether you will find this unfortunate gentleman in police records as a potential thief and housebreaker,' he told the constable who accompanied them to the mortuary, notebook at the ready. And as the clothes were removed from the body, 'Observe that he is well fed, and tolerably well groomed. Note that his face and lower arms are suntanned or weather beaten, also we may deduce from the fact that this tan continues below the collar line that he does not normally wear a cravat. His hands are calloused, but he is not, I fancy, a railroad worker or a labourer.'

As the shirt was removed, Faro continued, 'Note all the scratches on his lower arms. These swellings, are they insect bites, Vince? What would you deduce from that?'

'That he works out of doors, often with his sleeves rolled up,' said Vince triumphantly.

Faro nodded approvingly. 'I would hazard a guess, judging by the man's respectable appearance, that we have here a factor, a gamekeeper – someone of that class.'

Vince held up the jacket which they had removed from the corpse. 'I'm more interested in this, Stepfather. Feel it, such excellent material, certainly not the kind a labourer would wear.'

'Excellent, Vince lad, and you'll observe that it's of much better quality than his moleskin trousers or his boots. Nor, I suspect, considering our difficulties in taking it off him, was he its original owner.'

The body before them was now almost naked. 'His body linen too. Note that, Vince. Shabby but correct, no doubt influenced by his betters. So many of the poorer classes neglect to wear underdrawers.' Faro indicated the jacket again. 'Have you any ideas why our corpse should be wearing such an unsuitable garment as this?'

'Certainly not to work in. And I'd swear that he never set out with the least intention of climbing –', Vince emphasised the word, '– climbing Castle Rock or doing any violent activity in a jacket with sleeves three inches too short and so tight across chest and upper arms as to restrict all strenuous movement. He would have had extreme difficulty in lifting his arms above his head, let alone climbing . . .'

'Without undoing the buttons. See, a central one was torn off, probably in the fall. Well?'

'I know that look, Stepfather. You've already concluded that the poor unfortunate man was pushed off the Rock – or out of a window.' Resuming his examination of the body Vince continued, 'And that bruise to the back of his head was made by some blunt instrument, I suspect, before he fell.'

'Strange that his pockets yielded no information, that he carried not so much as a clay pipe with him. Consider the moustache and the unavoidable tobacco stains.'

Straightening up, Vince said, 'His body is amazingly unmarked. No scars, no evidence of bones broken in the past or operations. Hello, this is interesting. What do you make of this, Stepfather?' And he pointed to a tiny tattoo mark on the inside of the man's wrist. 'I almost missed that. What do you think it is?'

'A shamrock or a clover leaf, but rather imperfectly done. By the look of it, the work of an amateur. Poor devil. It didn't bring him much luck,' said Faro, and picking up the jacket he examined it closely. 'Observe that some of the buttons don't match and have been sewn on rather hastily with different-coloured thread. I rather suspect, lad, that this same jacket of excellent material has all the marks of being handed down – by some prosperous employer or deceased relative.'

'If that is the case, Stepfather, then I know from my boarding school and Medical College days that most Edinburgh tailors leave an identifying mark inside the lining. To assist with ordering of future garments by their rich customers, particularly clients who go to serve overseas, in the Colonial Service and so forth. They often prefer to order their tropical clothes and dress uniforms from a reliable home tailor. Let's see if I'm right.'

At the back of the neck, under the lining, were the marks he was searching for, 'K & J. 154/9'.

'K & J. Kennington and Jenner's,' said Vince. 'I'm a good customer in their gentlemen's outfitting department.

A visit to Mr Banks tomorrow should produce the name of the original owner.'

'Good lad. Meanwhile, we'll see what the constables bring back from Castle Rock. I may even go back anyway, and see what I can find.'

'Too dark for that kind of work now.'

'True.' Faro frowned. 'I'm for a walk up to the royal apartments while the trail is still warm. No, you go home, lad. Give them the usual excuses. Nothing scaring, detained at work and not to expect me in for supper. Be so good as to inform Mrs Brook to leave one of her cold collations. That will do me admirably. Well, what is it, lad?'

'Rose and Emily, Stepfather. This is their first night with us. I doubt whether they'll be willing to go to bed before Papa comes home. They'll certainly never go to sleep . . . '

'Then you must deputise for me.'

'Me? How?'

'You're the head of the house when I'm not around. What you do is read them stories, tuck them up in bed. Get in some practice for fatherhood. Might come in very useful some day.'

Vince groaned. 'God grant that "some day" is a million years away.' And consulting his pocket watch, 'As a matter of fact, Stepfather, I'm engaged to meet friends at Rutherford's within the hour. And I don't see how . . . '

Faro sighed impatiently. Domesticity was going to be damnably inconvenient with something in the offing that his every instinct told him was a case of murder.

Chapter Two

Sir Eric Haston-Lennard was an Orcadian who had been a good friend to Jeremy Faro's mother when her policeman husband was killed in Edinburgh. On retiral, with a knighthood, from the diplomatic service in India and Canada, appointed Keeper of Her Majesty's Historical Records in Scotland, he had been delighted to discover that young Jeremy was now Senior Detective Inspector Faro of the Edinburgh City Police.

A bachelor, fast becoming a recluse, Sir Eric had an apartment within the Castle, where Faro was always most cordially welcomed for a gossip, a dram and a hand at cards or chess. As befitted his illustrious role, where historical records existed of the long and turbulent history of Scotland and of Edinburgh in particular, Sir Eric's ability to track down ancient documents was of great assistance to the law.

Faro followed the uniformed guard along the cold stone corridor past the old royal lodging where unhappy, disillusioned Mary Queen of Scots sought refuge for her lying in. There, in a room not much larger than Mrs Brook's pantry, she had given birth to the future King James VI.

There was, however, nothing in the least melancholy about the large room into which Faro was ushered. The high walls were covered from wainscot to ceiling by an imposing gallery of paintings of Scottish monarchs. Neither historic nor contemporary, alas, they were the work of one imaginative artist, commissioned to impress the visiting monarch King George IV in 1822 with an imposing turnout of royal Stuart ancestors.

16

Announced, Faro thought the drawing room to be empty at first glance. No doubt Sir Eric would shortly appear from the direction of his study. Meanwhile he would enjoy the photographs of modern royalty, splendid examples of that new and magical art now taking Britain by storm. There was Sir Eric with Her Majesty and members of the royal family at Balmoral Castle. Again, Sir Eric in the uniform of the Queen's Royal Company of Archers being graciously received at Holyrood Palace. A silver-framed likeness held the place of honour. It showed Her Majesty in state robes and was signed, 'To Sir Eric, a devoted servant, Victoria R.'

'Inspector Faro?'

He put down the photograph guiltily and swung round to find the occupant of Sir Eric's high-backed chair had stepped into the candlelight. Faro was a little taken aback to find himself face to face not with his grizzled old friend, but with a very pretty girl in her early twenties. Now laying aside the book she held, she came forward, hand outstretched to greet him.

'How do you do? Sir Eric has been detained at Holyrood, I'm afraid, some boring royal business.'

Her handshake was strong and more to the point, it was surprising. Did she not know that etiquette demanded that well-bred young ladies should not touch a man's hand until they were formally introduced? Who the devil was she?

Bowing, he said, 'I'm so sorry to have inconvenienced you. I will return later. Perhaps you will tell Sir Eric when he arrives.'

'Wait. You're surely not going?'

'Well – yes.'

As Faro hesitated, she said eagerly, 'If you are not in a desperate hurry – please be my guest.' The invitation was accompanied by a winning smile.

'He should be here directly. And now, Inspector Faro, tell me all about yourself.' At Faro's startled expression, she said, 'We are not complete strangers you know. I have

17

heard so much about you – you are his clever policeman friend and I've been dying to meet you.'

Faro was surprised to find her on his own eye level. An inch over six foot, he was used to looking down on most of female kind but this girl, studying him so candidly, was almost as tall as himself.

Head on side, she continued, 'You don't look much like a detective, I must say. You look far too young – and jolly.'

Faro's feelings were far from jollity, if truth were to be told, however he was sufficiently vain to be flattered by the definition 'young' from a girl half his age.

'I've never met a detective, of course,' she said apologetically, 'and one gets very fixed ideas about people who are in authority. I've always imagined anyone to do with the Police Force as being quite stern and elderly.' She smiled, head on side. 'Not a bit like you. Sir Eric is always singing your praises and I'm so glad we've met at last.' And leaning forward confidentially, 'I'm terribly interested in crime.'

Faro's eyebrows raised a little at this frank and decidedly unfeminine admission. In respectable drawing rooms such matters were restricted to behind-hand whispers since any interest in improper behaviour was considered not only unwomanly, but wanton.

Here was a very forthright and unusual young female. And although he did not normally like tall women, finding that a certain aggressive manner went with the extra inches, this slender girl before him was most appealing. What Vince and his generation would undoubtedly call 'an absolute stunner'.

A stunner indeed, and enchantingly pretty. Raven-black tresses coiled on top of her head sloped to a widow's peak on her brow, emphasising a heart-shaped face and eyes that in candlelight seemed golden brown. Her figure was exquisite and he was wondering where she fitted into Sir Eric's lonely bachelor life, when she suddenly trilled with laughter at his expression.

'Oh, I am rude. Do pardon me. Of course, I should

have introduced myself. I'm Lucille Haston – Sir Eric is my uncle. I've been staying in Orkney with his sister, my Aunt Maud, and I guess I bullied the poor dear to let me come to Edinburgh.'

'You are from America?'

The girl clasped her hands and laughed delightedly. 'Bravo, Inspector – a good try. Actually I'm Canadian backwoods and Orkney isn't much better – a peevish, dull place.'

Faro refrained from comment. 'I hope Edinburgh is to your taste.'

'Not so far, alas.' She sighed. 'All we do is play cards or chess or read books. We never go anywhere. Absolutely no social life, no people of my own age – except the officers of the guard and Uncle says I can't associate with them, since I'm unchaperoned – except for my maid. And who wants to go out to dinner or to a ball accompanied by one's maid? Girls in the backwoods have a little more freedom, thank heaven . . .'

This breathless account was interrupted as the door was flung open by a uniformed maid, eyes discreetly lowered and carrying a tray.

Lucille Haston greeted her appearance with that trilling laugh.

'You see what I mean,' she said, and at the maid's sternly disapproving glance in the direction of this gentleman caller's boots, she sighed, 'No need to look like that, Bet. I am quite safe. Inspector Faro is a friend of Sir Eric's and he is also a policeman, so you needn't apply your eye to the keyhole any longer. I am totally in the hands of law and order and the Inspector is the very soul of propriety.'

Bet, embarrassed by her young mistress's declaration, bobbed a curtsy and, avoiding Faro's amused glance, hurried out.

'Refreshments, how nice. Will you take lemonade, or tea – and these biscuits are very good indeed.' At this hour of the day, Faro would have welcomed something stronger.

19

He eyed the sideboard with its decanters longingly. Sir Eric was very generous with his drams.

'I suppose you're wondering how my maid appeared with such alacrity.' And Lucille pointed to the large chimney-piece. 'Above that there is a small pantry which used to be the laird's lug in the old days,' she whispered. 'You know, the laird used to go up to his bedroom and listen in to what his guests were saying about him. Hardly the done thing, but very useful where chaperones are concerned.'

Taking a sip of lemonade, Faro asked, 'Are your parents abroad, Miss Haston?'

'Please call me Lucille. My parents? Both dead. In Canada – I was born there – when I was three, I can't even remember them. Uncle Eric is my guardian until I'm of age and meantime I live in Stromness with Aunt Maud, his unmarried sister. You know Stromness? Isn't it the dullest place ever?' she added.

'On the contrary; I'm very attached to Orkney. I lived near St Margaret's Hope and I sometimes miss it – and my family there – very much.'

'Surely not after living in divine Edinburgh all these years?' Lucille obviously regarded such an admission as incredible. 'Tell me about your family. I understand from Uncle that you're a widower. How sad – I am sorry.'

A sound of voices in the corridor and Faro was spared an account of his life story when the door opened to admit Sir Eric. Grey-haired, large and distinguished, he bore the unmistakable air of authority, the stamp of a Court official.

'My dear fellow, how good to see you. I trust my niece has been looking after you. What on earth is that she's given you to drink? For Heaven's sake, why didn't you ask her for a dram?'

'I wasn't sure – '

Lucille laughed. 'My dear fellow,' she said to Faro in a tolerable imitation of her uncle's manner, 'I know all about drams. Why, my dear Aunt Maud owns shares in the local distillery. You should have told me, silly man. You don't have to be polite with me.'

'That's quite enough, young lady. Thank you for entertaining the Inspector in my absence, but now you may retire. Now, Lucille,' he added in a threatening tone. 'Now – meaning immediately.'

Faro suppressed amusement for there was nothing in the least avuncular in this stern aristocrat's manner.

'But, Uncle . . . ' protested a sadly diminished Lucille.

'Now,' Sir Eric repeated firmly. He rose to his feet, a tall, regal, grey-haired disciplinarian. A sight to make strong men quail and more than a match for his spirited niece.

'It's been lovely to meet you,' said Lucille weakly. 'I hope I'll see you again before I leave,' she added with a sigh.

'Seeing that you're to be here until the autumn, I don't see how that can be avoided,' said Sir Eric, his good nature restored. His affectionate glance was followed by a threatening gesture. 'Now, be off with you, young lady. Good night, sleep well.'

'Good night, Uncle. Good night, Inspector.' A pretty curtsy and the door closed.

Handing Faro a dram, Sir Eric relaxed in the chair opposite. 'Hope she wasn't being too tedious. Bit of a rattle, but a sweet child really. Have to watch her with all these soldier lads about in the Castle. Seems to have no idea what men are like – well, you know what soldiers are. Given any encouragement, it could be deuced awkward.'

Drinking deeply, he sighed. 'We inherited her when a Vermont Haston cousin died. Time she had a husband. Her aunt's finding her a bit of a handful. Got this brilliant idea that there might be more chance of a good marriage here in Edinburgh. Perhaps when the Court comes to Holyrood. Anyway, I dare say you aren't here to talk about my niece. What can I do for you?'

'I'm not sure, Sir Eric. There was a body found at the base of Castle Rock . . . '

'So I've heard. Fellow trying to get into Queen Mary's

21

apartments. Up to no good, I warrant. Expect he was disturbed, panicked and tried to make his getaway. Good Lord, nobody's climbed down Castle Rock and got away with it since the wicked Earl of Bothwell back in the 1560s. Don't make men like that any more.'

'Have you any idea what he could have been looking for? Are there any valuables missing?'

'No, thank God. All safely locked in their glass cases. The rest of it is memorabilia – shoes, gloves, that sort of thing. Then there's a bed with hangings Mary embroidered personally.' He laughed. 'All authentic, dating from the sixteenth century, whether they belonged to the Queen or not.'

'I wonder if I could have a look round.'

'By all means. But you'll be wasting your time, lad. I know every item after all these years. Naturally when I heard about the intruder, first thing I did was to have them checked. Nothing missing, nothing even disturbed, I'm told. In fact, how he hoped to get in and out again is a mystery.'

Faro smiled and Sir Eric continued, 'Which, of course, is why you are here. Who was he, anyway?'

'We have no idea as yet.'

'I see. Well, you're more than welcome to have a search for any clues if you feel my men might have missed something vital. But you'll need to come back in tomorrow. Forster, who keeps the keys, is off duty, away to Haddington, I think. Returns in the morning. Now, time for a game of chess?'

'Not tonight, I'm afraid, sir. My mother has just arrived from Orkney with Rose and Emily – '

'Then I mustn't delay you.' With a sudden tender glance, he added, 'Compliments to your dear mother. It is far too long since we last met. Tell her I shall take the liberty of calling on her very soon.'

'Please do, Sir Eric. She would enjoy that.'

'You really think so?' He sounded eager. 'Such a splendid lady and one I have always held in the highest esteem.'

There was a suppressed sigh. 'We were very close after your father's death, you know.'

Faro did know, but not from Sir Eric. He had gathered from his mother's coy innuendoes that she might have married Sir Eric had she had the notion for a second marriage. But like her adored Queen Victoria she preferred to remain in love with the memory of a dead husband, relishing her widowhood to the full.

'Besides,' she told her son in a moment of confidence, 'it wasn't proper at all. I know my station in life, son, and it was not to be Lady Haston-Lennard. The very idea. What would my Orkney friends think of me, giving myself airs?'

'It's done every day in high society, Mother. Poor-born females are raised up by marriage.'

And now he was left wondering whether Mary Faro could possibly be the reason why Sir Eric had remained a bachelor.

'Do bring the little girls with you next time. I'd like to take them round myself. Tell them a bit of the history.'

'They would love that. They're full of stories about Queen Mary.'

'Good for them. I'll get my niece to go along too. Might stir her interest in the past. Our glorious history leaves her quite cold. All she cares for are pretty clothes and theatres and grand balls. Don't know what this young generation is coming to.'

Faro didn't feel inclined to argue that some of that young generation, like his doctor stepson Vince, were a credit to Scotland's future. At the door the two men shook hands.

'I'll expect you about ten tomorrow,' said Sir Eric.

'Thank you for your help, sir. And I'll bring the family on some later occasion.'

'Of course, of course. Crime and domesticity don't mix, do they?'

Rose and Emily Faro were early risers, so too was Faro's mother – the latter somewhat surprised, on preparing to indulge her son with the special treat of a breakfast tray, to find his bed slept in, but the room empty.

'He left the house half an hour ago, Mrs Faro,' the housekeeper told her. 'Quiet as a mouse he was. 'Spect he's gone for a constitutional. Oh yes, I'm sure he'll be back soon.'

Even as she spoke Faro was perched precariously on the Castle Rock. The point to which he had climbed was some eight feet above the spot where the body had been found. As he conducted his minute search of the area, he kept remembering those empty pockets.

Unless the dead man lived within walking distance, he must have had some money. And a clay pipe and tobacco in his pocket, since evidence had pointed to a smoker.

It was the stem of a clay pipe which led him to the discovery of a large knotted handkerchief, jammed in a crevice and almost hidden by gorse. Inside he found small coins and the pipe's bowl. He had guessed right. Its mode of transport had probably been the trouser pocket, since the hand-me-down jacket was such an uncommon tight fit.

Looking at these anonymous tokens, Faro almost missed the jewel completely. The sun, tardy in putting in an appearance, suddenly blazed forth from behind a bank of cloud. At that moment, Edinburgh's many churches, whatever their denomination, were more or less united in chiming forth the hour.

Eight, nine. Faro sighed. The search had taken longer than he had planned. It was hardly worth returning home for breakfast. He might as well go direct to the Castle, contact Forster and begin his investigations with a thorough search of Queen Mary's apartments.

It promised to be a glorious day, the sunlight swiftly drying the night's dewdrops in a kaleidoscope of delicate colour. Suddenly he strained forward for a closer look. This particular dewdrop was in fact the ruby and diamond glint of a jewel about three feet above his head.

Weighing it in his hand, he thought about the constables' method of investigation. Doubtless they had been conscientious enough but had used little imagination. They had searched below where the man was found, not realising that as a body rolled downwards, through such an uneven terrain of rocks and gorse, items carried in pockets could well be dislodged.

The jewel was a cameo pendant of delicate gold and enamel filigree surrounding a tiny miniature of a man in sixteenth-century apparel. The likelihood of it being 'buried treasure', lying here in this crevice for many years undiscovered, seemed very remote. The gold would have tarnished, in fact it was doubtful if that delicate filigree would have survived the passage of time.

Faro felt certain that the piece was authentic, valuable, and had found its way down the Castle Rock very recently. Looking up at the window of Queen Mary's apartments, he was now sure that the jewel he held had been connected with the man's violent death. When he walked round the glass cases shortly, Forster would confirm that one piece was missing.

There was a thrill of personal triumph in knowing that the mystery was beginning to unravel. In his hands he held the thread to the labyrinth, the very first clue. He was still certain that the scanty clues of the dead man's apparel pointed to his having been murdered, but why? A struggle on the heights with someone else who wanted to gain possession of the jewel? Was it that simple?

He should know part of the answer in ten minutes' time and could almost hear Sir Eric saying, 'Yes, of course. One of our treasures, belonged to Queen Mary. I know it well.'

I know it well. The imagined words repeated themselves over and over. I know it well. True, he knew little about jewellery, but what he now felt was the unmistakable sense of recognition. Just as he was certain that what he held was not a modern reproduction of an antique cameo, he was experiencing a feeling that raised the hairs on the back of his neck.

A sensation of times past. Of a happening far off but familiar too. At some other period in his life, he had held this piece in his hands. No, that could not be – one very like it. The remembrance brought with it a rush of guilt and shame. Someone had been very angry with him. His mother? Yes, his mother. No, she wasn't angry. She was upset – crying. And that made him feel terrible.

His fist tightened over the cameo. The possessor of a phenomenal memory, he fought desperately to remember. How, when and, most important, where?

At that moment, his glance took in a shadow moving far above him. Arms gesticulating? A large bird?

No. A black shape – hurtling down towards him.

He flattened himself against the rock and felt the wind of a huge dark object flying past him. A second later and it bounced, cracking, stone upon stone, past the very spot where he had been perched, to crash vibrating the railings far below.

His sudden evasive action dislodged the heath root supporting his weight. The next moment he too was hurtling down – down, the ground coming to meet him, dazzled in morning sunshine.

Chapter Three

Slithering painfully against every rock, Faro's downward progress was arrested with a sickening thud as he hit the ground and his ankle twisted under him.

He tried to stand. The pain was agonising. On hands and knees he crawled the short distance to the railings and stared helplessly through at the road with its bustling morning traffic, walkers and riders, carriages driving towards Princes Street and the West End.

'Help me, help me, please.' But the first passer by, a respectably dressed middle-aged woman walking with a small child, gave him a look of horror and speedily averted her eyes as if from some improper sight. Propelling the child along, ignoring shrill questions and backward glances, she hurried on, deaf and blind to his distress.

Next came three young girls, whispering and giggling as they walked arm-in-arm down the Wynd.

'Ladies, ladies. Please help me.' They slowed down momentarily. 'I'm a police officer,' he added desperately, trying to sound stern and convincing.

Hands on hips the trio regarded him. 'Don't look much like a policeman, does he?'

'Come away, Meg. He'll be one of those dafties, always tormenting decent folk.'

'Please listen,' Faro shouted as they moved away. 'If you won't help me, then tell the next constable you meet . . . '

But the three hurried on with occasional nervous backward glances and furious giggling, leaving Faro clinging miserably to the railings, staring after them. What a ridiculous predicament. Here he was, unable to climb the railings or walk in search of some exit. His hopes of getting anyone to help him steadily diminished – where, in heaven's name, were all Edinburgh's great God-fearing citizens who poured forth from churches each Sunday, eager with their good works?

'Help me please, I'm a police officer,' raised only looks of mocking merriment from a band of workmen.

'Serve you right,' they shouted across at him.

'Aye, hope you rot there.'

Could this nightmare be really happening to him, or would he awake in his bed in Sheridan Place? Now for the first time, he was experiencing a new dimension of crime. How easily attacks, even murders, could be accomplished in broad daylight without exciting more than a flicker of curiosity in passers by. Curiosity that might extend to perverse amusement at the victim's plight without arousing the slightest inclination to rush forward and offer assistance.

At last, the most welcome sight in the world, a police carriage trotting briskly up Johnston Terrace from the direction of the old King's Stables Road. At his frantic waving through the railings, the uniformed passenger jumped down; it was his assistant, and constant thorn in his side, Constable, lately promoted to Sergeant, Danny McQuinn.

The sight of his superior officer seemed to fill him with ill-suppressed merriment. 'Fancy finding you here, sir. Some young ladies said you'd been in the wars and needed help? Well, well – what did you do?'

'I had a slight argument with a falling rock,' Faro snapped and thought bitterly that the girls must have enjoyed relating their story to the handsome young policeman. He could just imagine them with their giggling, their flirtatious glances. Aye, McQuinn doubtless got considerably more of their anxious attention than he had done.

'Falling rock, eh, sir?' McQuinn gazed amused at the scene above them. 'There's a lot of it about, sir. Dangerous place for climbing.'

'I wasn't climbing, dammit. What do you think I was

doing – amusing myself? I was looking for a possible murder weapon.'

McQuinn shook his head sadly. 'You should leave that sort of thing to the young constables, sir.' His accompanying smirk and sidelong glance seemed to indicate that his superior officer had one injured foot in the grave already and the good one sliding dangerously.

'Dammit, man, someone has just tried to kill me.'

Danny McQuinn's eyes widened. 'Is that a fact? I hope you're making a charge, sir.'

'Get me out of here.'

'Can you walk, sir?'

'No, I can't walk. Otherwise I wouldn't be asking for help, would I?'

'I see. Just a moment.' And McQuinn produced from the closed interior of the carriage an extending ladder, part of the routine equipment for rescuing children who locked themselves in upstairs rooms, and for reaching old ladies' cats who got themselves stranded in trees. It was also useful for saving folks who fell into the water – by accident, not intent.

With the help of the driver of the carriage and a considerable amount of painful effort on Faro's part, the two men managed to get him over the railings and hoisted inside the cab.

'Quite comfortable now, are you, sir?'

Faro forbore to reply. His gratitude for the rescue was now exceeded by feelings of humiliation and resentment of his dependence upon the hated McQuinn. At that moment he would have enjoyed nothing more than soundly boxing his ears. Fortunately for McQuinn, he needed that spare hand to support himself in the swaying carriage.

'Anything I can do for you, sir?'

'Yes, you can take me home,' snapped Faro and decided to keep the clues he had discovered to himself. He was furious, in no condition now to search the royal apartments, and if his ankle was broken, as he feared from its throbbing agony, then Vince, in his new role of qualified doctor, would doubtless immobilise him for some time.

Meanwhile a verdict of 'death by misadventure' would be recorded on the dead man whose body, if unclaimed, would go to the medical students. As for his murderer, the law would be cheated again as the trail grew dim and finally disappeared before Faro was fit to resume his investigations.

Sitting back in the carriage, with McQuinn's shrill whistling of an Irish jig adding insult to his injury, Faro realised his accident had made abundantly evident that it was an assassin he was up against. And a desperate one at that, who would attack in broad daylight – he remembered that glimpse of upraised arms against the sky, and the projectile, too well aimed to be an accident.

His search had been observed and noted by his adversary, to whom an encounter with 'falling' rock must have suggested a convenient way of disposing of this inquisitive policeman. Only the presence of what some might call a guardian angel, which was to Jeremy Faro a tangible awareness of lurking danger, had saved his life. He shuddered. But for this uncanny sixth sense, which had paid off many times in his long career, he would now be lying alongside the dead man in the city mortuary.

At last McQuinn delivered him like a large and unwieldy piece of furniture to his own front door. If Faro had thought that his injury was the worst that could happen to him, then he had not bargained for the hysterical behaviour of the four females occupying his home. At that moment he was grateful that three of them were there on a purely temporary basis.

Fuss was a part of Mrs Brook's nature that Faro was teaching her sternly to keep in check. The housekeeper was, however, totally outclassed by his mother, with whom he could do nothing at all.

He only thanked God that he had made light of the incident. He had slipped and fallen, that was all. If Mary Faro had an inkling that the 'accident' had been deliberate then he would have to endure once again the story

30

of 'your poor dear father's' unfortunate death. The long and tortuous account of the events which had widowed his young wife and left their one child fatherless would be retold, complete with tears still remarkably fresh and ready flowing after thirty years.

Rose and Emily were speedily infected by the panic and confusion. Taking their cue from Grandmama, they rushed up and downstairs, 'helping' with basins of hot water which they contrived to spill.

The atmosphere was one of utter chaos when Vince put his key in the front door. Dealing with this chorus of lamentations at amazing speed, he removed Faro into the surgery and closed the door very sweetly but firmly on the hand-wringing female members of his family.

To Vince's enquiry, 'How did this happen?' Faro replied, 'On Castle Rock. Stepped back too smartly. Didn't realise I was so far off the ground.' So disgusted was he by the morning's farcical events, and in general with the whole business, that he grumpily resolved to keep his suspicions of an assassin to himself.

Truth to tell, he couldn't bear one more mocking, disbelieving glance. Especially from Vince, who merely nodded, removing the boot from his stepfather's bruised and rapidly swelling ankle as gently as possible. 'Well, was it worth it? Did you find any clues?'

Mollified, from his pocket Faro brought forth the clay pipe and the handkerchief with its coins.

'That doesn't tell us very much, Stepfather. Hardly worth an injured ankle.'

'But I also found this.' And savouring his triumph, Faro handed him the Queen Mary cameo.

Vince turned it over. 'Looks very old. Are those real rubies and diamonds, do you think?'

'I do. Realise what this means, lad?'

'You think the dead man dropped it. And that he'd stolen it from the royal apartments?'

'I was about to check that with Sir Eric when this

31

damned thing happened.' And watching Vince minutely examine the jewel, he continued, 'Tell me, do you recognise it?'

Vince shook his head. 'No. Should I?'

'Think hard, lad. You're sure you've never seen one like this before?'

'Quite sure, Stepfather. Why do you ask?'

'Because when I found it I thought that I had. That sometime I'd held a jewel exactly like this in my hands.'

Vince shook his head. 'Then it must have been long before we met.' Producing bandages from the cupboard, he said. 'By the way, I went to Kennington & Jenner's. At the crack of nine, I presented myself to Mr Banks. He was very disappointed when he learned that I wasn't wanting a tropical outfit . . . '

'The jacket – what did he say?' Faro interrupted impatiently, biting his lip at the pain as Vince gently manipulated his ankle.

'Some little success, Stepfather. The admirable Mr Banks checked the reference number in his little book and found that it was made specially for a very good customer, Sir James Piperlee – his place is near Glencorse.'

'Well done, lad. When do we go? Ouch!'

'Sorry, Stepfather, I'm being as gentle as I can.'

'Broken, is it?'

Vince laughed. 'Of course not. Bad sprain, that's all. You'll be right as rain in a couple of weeks. But you're to keep off it until then. Rest's the only cure.'

'Rest? And what about Sir James Piperlee?'

'Oh, I dare say he'll still be around.'

'We're wasting valuable time, lad.'

Vince went on with his bandaging. 'Nature has laid down through the ages her own rules regarding healing flesh – and that includes broken bones and sprained ankles. She has her own timetable for everything. There are no exceptions and she can't be hurried. So, like other mortals, Stepfather, you must learn to bear it all patiently as possible . . . '

'Look, you've said it was just a sprain,' Faro interrupted irritably. 'A sprain's nothing serious, but this is bloody painful. Are you sure you've got it right?'

Vince sat back on his heels and regarded his stepfather candidly. A moment later he went again to the cupboard and returned with the brandy bottle.

'Just exactly what I need,' said Faro with a sigh.

'Yes, and in this instance purely medicinal, so don't enjoy it too much. You're fairly shaken, aren't you?' And as Faro handed him back the empty glass, 'I suspect that you're not telling me everything. You're not usually careless, or prone to step off rocks without first looking right and left very cautiously. So how about telling me exactly what happened, and how you came by this? The truth now – did you fall – or were you pushed?'

'A rock was hurled down at me. I stepped aside – and fell. Someone tried to kill me, lad.'

While Faro filled in the details, Vince completed his bandaging in silence.

'That's it, then. As far as I can go, Stepfather. The rest is up to you.'

Thanking him, Faro tried to stand up. When he swore, Vince grinned.

'Don't take it out on me, Stepfather.'

'It's damnably sore.'

'Give it time.'

'Time! And don't you go round blabbing what I've told you to them,' said Faro with a fierce nod towards the closed door.

'You must think I'm a fool. Two ladies with the vapours and two hysterical little girls. Life, for us mere men, would hardly be worth living. Anyway, you should be jolly thankful that it wasn't your neck. I expect that was the intention – a more fatal area, I assure you, that doesn't respond to healing with time.'

'Hold on, this bandage – it is too bloody tight.'

'Tight is what it has to be, if it's to get better, so do stop complaining, there's a good fellow.'

Faro seized his boot, and watched by Vince finally gave up the unequal struggle to get it fastened.

'How am I expected to do anything if I can't get a boot on and I can't walk?'

Vince grinned. 'The answer is simple. You don't even try.'

'God dammit.'

'Precisely – and all criminals too. You'll have to let them rest for a while.'

'Damnation – are you certain about this ankle?'

'Oh indeed I am, Stepfather. Allow me to know a badly sprained limb when I see one. And if you want a second opinion I can get Dr Kellar to look at it. As Police Surgeon, he's more used to handling the dead than the living, of course, so don't expect him to be as gentle as I am.'

Seeing Vince's offended expression, Faro patted his arm. 'Sorry, lad, but it is a cursed nuisance, you must admit.'

'I dare say you'll get quite adept at hopping up and downstairs,' said Vince with a cheerful grin. 'A sprightly man like you.'

Faro gave him a sharp glance. 'Thank you for not reminding me I'll soon be forty – at the moment, McQuinn's favourite taunt.'

'Really, Stepfather. You're getting as sensitive as a dowager about your age. Forget it. Probably McQuinn envies you that abundant head of hair – as I do. I reckon I'll get half an inch more face to wash with every passing year,' said Vince with a rueful glance in the mirror. 'Besides, you've got good bones, a fine strong Viking face, a splendid figure and an excellent constitution – barring regrettable accidents like typhoid and sprained ankles, which can happen to anyone. You're really wearing very well,' he added sternly. 'And you don't need my assurances that you don't look your age.'

'As a matter of fact, you're the second person to tell me so in the past twenty-four hours,' said Faro smugly.

'Good.'

To continue was irresistible. 'Yes, indeed. The first was a very pretty young lady – not much more than "sweet and twenty".'

His stepson's weakness for any female young and pretty was immediately kindled and at the end of Faro's story of his meeting with Lucille Haston, Vince stressed how anxious he was to help. His fervent offer of assistance, by taking his injured stepfather's place on a personally conducted tour of the royal apartments, was too eager not to be also quite transparent.

'Sounds like a splendid idea, lad, if you can manage my mother, Rose and Emily too,' said Faro carelessly. Seeing Vince's doubtful look, he added, 'I'd really be grateful. As you know, they're longing to visit the Castle and I honestly haven't the least idea about entertaining little lasses.'

This admission put Vince on his mettle. 'Really, Stepfather, where the family is concerned, you certainly don't appear to exercise that famous logic of yours.'

'And what do you mean by that?' asked Faro indignantly.

'Why, they leave clues everywhere about what they like. All very easy to follow. Even I, who am no detective, can interpret the desires of little girls to perfection. Mind you,' he added with a rueful grin, 'I'm not always quite so astute where their older sisters are concerned.'

In the days that followed, Faro discovered the advantages of being a temporary invalid. With injured ankle resting on a stool, he was the centre of attention. The entire household pivoted around him, making him once again conscious of all that he had lost of the joys of parenthood. He also recognised that this unexpected and enforced inactivity was a small blessing in disguise. Miraculously, it had drawn him closer to his little daughters than he had been since their mother died.

And even when Lizzie was alive, how uncomplaining she had been of his constant neglect, his shortcomings as husband and father. How humbly she accepted his dedication to the Edinburgh City Police and all that being a detective entailed. His duty was never to be questioned, and must come always ahead of wife and family.

It was not until he heard his mother in his study upstairs, a shrill note of protest in her voice as she talked to Mrs Brook, that the spell of domestic harmony was broken at last.

Chapter Four

Stirred into action and spurred on by indignation, Faro found that he was now able to hop upstairs quite rapidly.

His study, that holy of holies, was in mortal danger. Hadn't Mrs Brook warned his mother that it was sacrosanct? That no woman was ever permitted, without his consent and supervision, to cross its threshold armed with broom, duster and intention to make clean and tidy the desk with its heaps of papers and documents, the piled up volumes on the floor. To the casual eye the sight was chaotic, but Faro knew the precise location of everything, and exactly where to lay hands on that vital information he was seeking.

Breathlessly reaching the landing, he was met by the indignant and reproachful face of his diminutive mother. With her rosy cheeks, her sharp black eyes and hair untouched by grey, she looked for all the world like an angry robin prepared to defend her territory.

Before he could open his voice to protest, she shook her fist at him defiantly.

'Jeremy Faro, you should be ashamed of yourself.' And pointing to the open study door, 'To think that a son of mine should live like this. Such a rat's nest in there as I never saw in my whole life.' And turning to Mrs Brook, who looked extremely uncomfortable and embarrassed at having to witness her illustrious employer's chastisement, Mrs Faro added sternly, 'It wasn't the way he was brought up by me. Oh dear no. I just don't know where to begin . . . '

'I don't expect you to begin – anywhere, Mother,' Faro interrupted coldly. When she looked as if the ready tears were about to overflow, he added hastily, 'You're here on holiday, remember.'

'Holiday or not, rooms have to be kept clean and tidy. Do you think I can rest easily downstairs now that I've actually seen spiders cavorting – over there – in the corners? And I shouldn't be surprised if there's worse than spiders,' she said with a shudder.

'And what's wrong with spiders, I should like to know? Remember Robert the Bruce.'

'Now don't you give me your clever talk, son. Mrs Brook will bring up her feather duster and we will set to work immediately.'

As the housekeeper gratefully disappeared downstairs, Mrs Faro marched into the study and tried in vain to reach the high shelf. 'And now if you'll just push across that footstool, I'll get down your poor dear Papa's hamper.'

'I'll do that, Mother.'

'Very well.' And dusting her fingers she added accusingly, 'From the grime on it, I don't suppose you've even looked inside since I sent it down from Orkney.'

'I haven't had time, Mother. I've been rather busy this summer.'

'Then you should have made time. First things first, that's what we've always said in our family. And your poor dear father, he would have wanted you to show a little interest in his work, and respect for his memory. Especially when you took after him so greatly and went to be a policeman.'

Once again, Faro was torn between guilt and irritation at his mother's reproaches on the subject of his 'poor dear father'. Constable Magnus Faro had been thus immortalised by his devoted widow, ever since the day he met his death making his way homeward at the end of a night's duty with the Edinburgh City Police.

Being run over and fatally injured at night on Edinburgh's

steep, cobbled High Street made treacherous by rain and fog was not unknown in the annals of the city. But according to Mary Faro, her husband's death was no accident. She insisted that it was deliberate murder, although no one would listen or give credence to her wild accusations, and her indignation burned undimmed by the passing of more than thirty years for that death unavenged.

Jeremy had been nearly five. And looking back, he realised that his mother's hero worship of her dead husband, those epic tales of his marvellous exploits, had filled their son's earliest days with only a burning desire to leave Orkney. For as long as he could remember Jeremy Faro's one unswerving ambition had been to go to the mainland and follow in the footsteps of his illustrious father.

When at eighteen he left, Mary saw glumly that her enthusiasm for her late husband had badly misfired and life in the Edinburgh City Police was not what she had ever imagined or intended for her only son. More than anything else, she had wanted to keep him near her, to see him settled down on a croft like his forebears. They had been farmers since the sixteenth century, when a Royal Stuart bastard had given a piece of land to the female Sinclair he had already bestowed twins upon.

'Have you never even been curious to read all those notebooks your dear father kept?' asked Mary Faro. 'Every one of his cases, he would sit up writing half the night. "Getting the facts straight", he called it,' she added proudly.

Jeremy didn't answer as he considered how best to transfer the hamper into some prominent position that would placate her. He had no wish to stress his neglect by confessing that he wasn't much of a reader of police reports. He'd seen and participated in too many in his twenty years as a policeman and, as far as he was concerned, they made very dry reading for an off-duty hour.

Inspector Faro preferred his crime to be of the fictional variety, in the swashbuckling adventures of Sir Walter

Scott's novels, the marvellous mysteries of Charles Dickens. Especially the latter, based on fact and a criminal element in London which had its counterpart in Edinburgh too. The intimate knowledge Mr Dickens displayed showed how well he understood crime and the courts of justice. How Jeremy admired and envied his talent to write such highly readable and entertaining novels where – unlike real crime or anything resembling life itself – virtue was always triumphant, with all the mysteries solved and all the loose ends tied together in a most satisfying way on the very last page.

Jeremy's deepest regret was that he was still a child in Orkney when Mr Dickens was given the freedom of Edinburgh in 1841. How wonderful to have heard the great writer reading from his own works and how infinitely sad, like losing a friend, to read of his recent death.

As he eased the hamper from its lofty perch, his mother hovered anxiously. 'Are you sure you can manage? It can wait until Vince gets home,' she added helpfully.

Vince might not arrive until evening and the thought of being gently nagged on the subject of spiders and general untidiness set Jeremy's teeth on edge. Better to keep her quiet with her feather dusters.

'Of course I can manage. It isn't all that heavy. Just a lot of papers,' he said cheerfully. However, he had reckoned without the footstool that lurked behind him. Stepping backwards, he staggered against it, lost his balance and both he and the hamper landed heavily in a painful collision with the nearby sofa.

'Oh your poor leg,' said his mother. 'I hope you haven't made it worse.'

Faro, wincing with renewed pain, made light of the subject, grateful that her first thoughts had been for him, since the hamper had been even less fortunate in its encounter with the sofa's wooden back.

'Oh dear, oh dear, just look at that now,' said Mrs Faro, transferring her attention to its broken lid. Hanging forlornly by one hinge, it had burst open, spewing papers everywhere over the well-polished floor. 'No, son, you stay where you are, I'll get them.'

Jeremy sank down thankfully on to the sofa as the noise brought Rose and Emily on to the scene. They added their lamentations, their offers to bring Papa a glass of water, while Jeremy rubbed the sore skin of his injured ankle. Weakly he suggested that they would be better employed assisting their Grandmama, down on her hands and knees, retrieving the hamper's contents and considerably hindered by the playful Rusty, who regarded anyone on the floor as fair game.

Soon all three were reverently gathering together the yellowing notes that had burst out of covers, and papers tied with tape. A new sound was added, his mother's barely suppressed sniffs, as if it had been only yesterday that she had laid her dearest Magnus in his grave.

As she retied the bundles and kissed each one, Jeremy watched in amazement, and some envy, that any love could be sustained so long or so deeply.

Rose and Emily, kneeling beside her, exchanged help-less glances with their father over her head. At a nod from him, rightly interpreted, they saw immediately what was needed. They hugged and kissed and petted their grandmother, while she dabbed at her eyes and called them her 'wee darlings' and apologised for being so weak.

At last all the documents were tidily restored to the hamper, the girls bringing additional contributions which had slithered over the polished floor and had vanished, with Rusty in hot pursuit, under the less accessible pieces of furniture.

Before closing the damaged lid, Mrs Faro withdrew one packet. 'If you ever feel inclined to read any of your dear father's cases, I urge you to look at this one. His very last, the one he was working on when he was murdered.' And touching the faded ribbon tenderly, 'I tied these papers together myself on the day he was buried,' she said sadly, 'with the bow from my wedding bouquet.'

Jeremy glanced at his father's neat handwriting.

'"The Mysterious Corpse of a Baby Discovered in the Wall of Edinburgh Castle. 1837",' he read. 'Sounds intriguing.'

Mrs Faro nodded. 'Yes, it does and I curse the day he ever became involved in it. Mark my words, son, I would not have been a widow all these lonely years, had he left well alone.' With a sigh she added, 'I still remember as if it were yesterday, just a few weeks after our dear Queen came to the throne it was, he came home so excited about some secret he thought he'd discovered. What it was we'll never know now.'

Two hours later it was a vastly improved study that Faro entered, cleaned and tidied with a gratifying lack of any disturbance to his papers and books. His mother, on whom he had lavished abundant praise, was now taking a well-earned afternoon rest and the house was silent but for the poignant song of a blackbird in the garden mingled with his daughters' faint laughter downstairs.

Faro sighed. He was rarely at home at this hour of the day and there was undoubtedly a most agreeable sense of repose and wellbeing in the domestic sounds of a summer afternoon. His investigations into the death of an unknown man lying in the city mortuary seemed remote and unimportant, along with his own monstrous suspicions that only days ago he had been the victim of a murderous attack.

Afternoons like this, tranquil with sunshine, resplendent with birdsong, convinced a man of his own immortality. Small wonder the general populace of a respectable Edinburgh preferred to believe that crime and sudden death were none of their business, and he could find it in his heart to forgive their indifference to his plight on Castle Rock.

He wondered how Vince had fared in his mission to

the Castle. He had promised, if Dr Kellar released him in time, to take the cameo to Sir Eric and have its theft from the glass cases in the royal apartments confirmed. For once, Faro was quite happy to leave the routine investigation in his stepson's capable hands and decided that he might well profit from this unexpected break in his busy life by reading up his father's last case.

The connection with Edinburgh Castle intrigued him and a casual skimming of the notes, left incomplete at Constable Magnus Faro's death, revealed that a tiny coffin containing the remains of a child had been found by workmen, entombed in the wall of the royal apartments.

How had it got there and why? Here was a mystery worthy of Sir Walter Scott himself, thought Jeremy, but hardly the reason for foul play outside the imaginative realms of fiction. Even if his father's accident had been deliberate, and he had always been rather doubtful about that, it was hard enough solving crimes that happened last week or last month. There was no possible way of solving a thirty-three-year-old mystery.

Faro came back to the present to the sound of voices upraised. Of shrill screams – issuing forth from the same region where only a short time ago had drifted his daughters' delighted laughter.

His peace broken, resentfully he opened the study door.

'Girls – Emily, Rose –' his mother's voice was added to the noise. 'Stop it at once. Stop. Jeremy – Jeremy, come and do something about your children.'

Reluctantly emerging, he saw his mother's angry and flustered countenance.

Clutching the banister, he limped downstairs. 'What's all this about, Mother? Can't you deal with it?'

'No. They need a father's discipline.'

Pushing open the door, he saw Rose and Emily rolling on the floor, fighting, clawing, screaming. Faro groaned inwardly. His little girls, happy and laughing, were angelic. Quarrelling had made them into ugly little monsters, charging his serene and comfortable bachelor existence, his retreat from the world of sordid crime and violence, with exactly the sort of unpleasant domestic situation he most dreaded.

'Rose – Emily – please . . . ' His command went quite unheeded. Even to his own ears, it sounded most ineffectual.

'I'm the princess and you're my wicked stepmother.'

'I'm not. I'm not.'

'You are.'

'I'm older than you – and I get to wear it.'

'Oh no you don't. I want it. I found it.'

'You promised turns.'

'You've had your turn, now I want it back. It's mine.'

'It is not.'

'It is.'

'You wicked liar. I found it on the floor.'

'I hate you. You're cruel and horrid.'

'I would cut off your head if I had half a chance.'

'You little beast – beast . . . '

As the two fell upon each other with renewed frenzy, Jeremy entered the fray and separated them with difficulty, trying desperately to keep his injured leg away from flailing arms and legs as they tried to kick each other.

'Girls – girls! Stop this at once. Are they often like this?' he asked his mother desperately. 'You told me they never quarrelled.'

'They don't. I can't understand it. Something must have upset them,' she said, clutching Emily while Jeremy seized the opportunity to hold Rose in a firm grip.

Red faced, tear stained, the two girls stared mutinously at each other.

'Now, behave and say you're sorry to your sister, Rose.'

'Shan't!'

'Oh yes you will, if you want any supper tonight.'

'Don't want any.'

'Very well. You will stay in your room – no Arthur's Seat with Vince tomorrow.'

'And no Edinburgh Castle either,' Mrs Faro added for good effect.

The two girls looked thoughtful and distinctly mollified at this punishment.

Then Rose shook her head defiantly. 'All right, I'll behave, if that's what you want, Papa.'

'I do indeed. And you can begin by saying you're sorry to your sister. Ouch – what was that? What have you got in your hand?'

Rose immediately put her hand behind her back.

'Let me see. Come now . . . '

'It's a brooch. I found it.'

'No, she didn't, Papa. I found it,' yelled Emily.

'Never mind who found it. Give it to me – at once.'

And Rose placed in her father's hand a familiar cameo, the Queen Mary jewel which should, at that very moment, have been with Vince on its way to Edinburgh Castle.

'You stole this from your stepbrother, didn't you?' Rose trembled at her father's angry expression. 'Didn't you, you wicked child?'

'I did not,' was her brave reply.

'Oh yes, you did. Rose – and Emily – I am ashamed of you.'

'So that's what you were quarrelling about,' said Mrs Faro. 'You naughty, naughty children. Your Papa has you here for a holiday and you repay him by stealing things.'

'We didn't steal anything, Papa. We – or rather I – found it on the floor, under the table in your study. Rusty was playing with it . . . '

'What a dreadful lie. Really, Emily.'

'It isn't a lie.'

'It's true, Papa,' said Emily, now staunchly coming to her sister's defence. 'It was after we helped gather up the papers . . . '

'And there's no use protecting one another now. It's too late for that,' said Mrs Faro. 'I'd never have believed the two of you were capable of such wickedness.'

'But we didn't do anything wrong . . . '

'Honestly, Grandma . . . '

'Let me see that, will you, Jeremy? Oh dear, oh dear.' Mary held it in her hand, and then with a shudder, she handed it back.

'You've seen it before, Mother?' Jeremy looked again. At first glance identical to the cameo he had found on Castle Rock, there was a difference. The tiny miniature in its centre was not of a man, but of a woman in sixteenth-century dress.

'Aye, I've seen it before, lad,' said his mother. 'Your poor dear father came across it during his last case. When he was killed. It might even be the reason why he was killed. I never wanted to see it again. That's why I put it in the hamper with that letter.'

'What letter, Mother?'

'From some antique dealer he knew – an old man in the High Street.'

'What did it say?' asked Faro eagerly.

'Oh, I don't know. I can't remember. All I know is it was too late to save my poor love,' she added with a sniff. 'There was a curse on it – and there still is. Look how it turned our two darlings into wee devils, tearing at each other's throats,' she ended dramatically.

'This is the envelope that it fell out of, Papa,' said Rose, taking a crumpled packet out of her pinafore pocket. 'You see, Papa, we weren't lying,' she added triumphantly, taking Emily's hand.

'And we didn't steal anything from anyone, did we, Rose?'

'Rusty found it under the desk.'

'It was so pretty we only wanted to play with it while Grandma was resting and you were busy in your study.'

From the envelope Jeremy withdrew the antique dealer's letter.

Dear Magnus: This is undoubtedly an interchange-able piece of jewellery particularly popular in the sixteenth century in the Court circles, when the monarch would give one part to a particular favourite as a love token, bearing his or her likeness. Also among wealth noble families, for sentimental reasons, parts were exchanged between lovers and parents/children. There are usually two or more pieces which can be worn separately or together as a pendant. In my opinion, this work dates from the mid-1500s and as the miniature is undoubtedly of Queen Mary may indeed have originated from her collection of jewels.

Incidentally, the rubies and diamonds are authentic, making this a very valuable piece. I am intrigued to know more of its history. When next we meet you must tell me how you came by it – I am, Your obedient servant, Chas. Pilter.

There had been no next meeting. The letter was dated 3 August 1837, the day after Magnus Faro died. The address, 'Fayre's Wynd, High Street', and presumably Mr Pilter had both vanished a generation ago.

'That lady in the little painting, Papa. I've been thinking,' said Rose, looking over his shoulder, 'isn't she like the drawing we have at home of Queen Mary?'

Jeremy looked at his daughter approvingly. Rose might be only a child, but he was pleased to note that already she showed signs of having inherited his keen powers of observation.

Queen Mary. And the matching cameo, he was certain, would prove to be a portrait of her consort, Lord Darnley, to be worn together or separately as the antique dealer had said.

'Well done, Rose,' he murmured approvingly.

'Am I right, Papa?' she beamed at him.

Hugging her to his side, he asked his mother, 'Didn't you know this might be valuable?'

Mrs Faro shuddered. 'All I knew was that it brought bad luck. It had taken your poor dear father. I never wanted to see it again.'

47

And listening to her, Jeremy Faro heard another echo from the past and knew why the jewel he had found on Castle Rock had been so tantalisingly familiar. Memory clicked into place and presented a small boy whose curiosity had led him to the mysterious hamper so revered by his mother. Caught with the forbidden cameo in his hand, he was scolded severely. He remembered her anger clearly, her tears and his desolation, his fears of God's wrath for naughty children.

What did it all mean? Where was the vital link? For the facts remained. The two pieces had indeed brought a trail of destruction. His own father, Constable Magnus Faro, had died. More than thirty years later a mystery man had also died. And, but for the grace of God, Jeremy Faro himself would have been the third victim.

His mother called it cursed. That label was too easy for Faro, who was not a superstitious man. His logical mind refused to accept the existence of curses. If they existed, then he believed they were brought about by man alone, by his folly and greed, which had a habit of rebounding upon him.

He could hardly wait for Vince's return, but with his daughters forgiven, kissed and cuddled and rewarded with goodies from Mrs Brook's inexhaustible supply, Faro decided to read carefully his father's notes.

Somewhat cynically, remembering how he had found clues and the cameo overlooked by the police searchers on Castle Rock, he decided that tomorrow, with Vince's aid and a walking stick, he was now fit enough to go out to the Piperlees estate. To interview the laird, Sir James, on the subject of the dead man's jacket.

And then he would go up to the Castle and take a careful look around the royal apartments. Trust no one, not even your own first observations. Check and double check, was a motto that had served him well in the past.

But as he climbed the stairs to his study, although

the sun shone brilliantly, he shivered as if a cloak of
ice had been thrown around him. He knew the feeling
well. It was his demon, his own personal premonition
of disaster.

Chapter Five

In his study, his door closed with the warning that he was not to be disturbed, Faro began to read his father's notes.

'The Mysterious Corpse of a Baby Discovered in the Wall of Edinburgh Castle. 1837.'

Constable Magnus Faro had been thorough. In his neat, precise handwriting, 'Copied from the *Scotsman*, 11 August 1830,' Jeremy read:

Sensational Historic Discovery

Two workmen, engaged on renovating the royal apartments at Edinburgh Castle after a fire, have made the gruesome discovery of a tiny coffin. Nearly in line with the Crown Room and about six feet from the pavement to the quadrangle, the wall was observed to return a hollow sound when struck.

On removing a block of stone, a recess was discovered measuring about 2 feet 6 by 1 foot, containing the remains of a child enclosed in an oak coffin, evidently of great antiquity and very much decayed. Wrapped in a shroud, a cloth believed to be woollen, very thick and somewhat resembling leather, and within this the remains of a shroud of a richly embroidered silk and cloth of gold which suggested some portion of a priest's vestment, most likely used in the Masses secretly held in Queen Mary's oratory.

Such a sanctified garment would be approved as suitable for the interment of one of royal blood, a little prince, born and baptised in the Popish faith, rather than for the hasty disposal of some Court lady's indiscretion. Further evidence being two initials wrought upon the shroud, one alas, was indecipherable, but the other, the letter 'J', was distinctly visible.

From the coffin's concealment in the wall, secrecy of the closest character was evidently the object, and being wainscoted thereafter, no trace remained.

By order of the Castle officials the remains were restored to the coffin and the aperture closed up.

Attached was a further newspaper cutting, dated 12 July 1837.

Egyptian-Style Curse in Edinburgh Castle.

Two workmen, Matthew O'Hara and John Femister, died tragically when the high scaffolding on the battlements of Edinburgh Castle collapsed under them. A third man, Peter Dowie, suffered serious injuries. All three had been engaged for renovation work on the inside of the royal apartments and when the old panelling was removed in line with the Court room and near the quadrangle, the workmen's attention was drawn to a loose stone just above their heads. Further investigation revealed the presence of a child's coffin which had been interred behind the wainscoting a short distance from the bedchamber where, on 19 June 1566, Queen Mary gave birth to the future King James VI (and I of England), the only issue of her marriage to Lord Darnley.

Following upon the recent suicide of Colonel Theodore Lazenby, the officer in charge of Castle renovations, the accidental deaths of the two workmen irresistibly raise the question in the minds of gullible and superstitious persons, as to whether these unfortunate happenings were mere coincidence, or the fulfilment of an Egyptian-style curse for disturbing the dead?

It is now almost seven years (August 1830) since

51

the original discovery was made. Then as now misfortune and death struck the unhappy individuals who disturbed the oak coffin containing an infant's mummified remains. Reverently reinterred, this gruesome mystery from Queen Mary's tragic reign has lain undisturbed until last week when repairs and renovations were ordered to make all in good order and readiness for Her Majesty Queen Victoria's first visit to her Scottish kingdom since she ascended to the throne last month.

Concerning the deceased. A full obituary of Colonel Lazenby, a distinguished officer and gentleman who was recently married, is to be found on page 2. Of the two workmen who died, Mr John Femister, aged 35, from Leith, is a widower with one daughter. O'Hara, aged about 23, an itinerant labourer, is believed to hail from Ireland, as is Dowie who sustained serious head and back injuries and has been admitted to the Infirmary.

Attached to the newspaper account was Colonel Lazenby's obituary, a glowing tribute to his service at home and abroad in India and Canada. Magnus Faro had underlined heavily that he was the only son of Lord and Lady Phineas Lazenby, Aberdale, East Lothian.

Magnus Faro's report followed. Of how he had been on duty in the High Street when the scaffolding collapsed. He had raced to the scene, where he had found two men already dead and one so critically injured as to be near death. His account continued:

My attempts to investigate the accident further were impeded by Colonel Lazenby and other army officials who refused to allow me to proceed, in the interests of my own safety, and insisted that I inform the Central Office immediately and return with other constables to assist me. By the time I returned, half an hour later, the debris was in the final stages of being carted away and the dead men were on their way to the mortuary. I realised, of course, that any evidence, of negligence or of unsafe timber and ropes, if such existed, had also been lost.

The report went on:

Later:

I am very sceptical about Egyptian-style curses. The two men who died in 1830 were drowned, washed ashore at Granton. It was thought they had purloined a boat which capsized. Their names were Connor and Doyle, 'believed to be from Ireland' (like most itinerant labourers, poor starving wretches who arrive in droves from Ireland and the Highlands). Christian names would have been a help for further investigation, but employers of casual labour are frequently careless about such details.

Notes:

Tomorrow I intend to see Dowie (if he is still alive and capable of speech) then proceed to Leith and talk to Femister's relatives.

On another sheet of paper, hastily scrawled:

Tried to see Dowie, but he is far gone.
Was the cameo buried in the child's coffin?

Jeremy felt the surge of excitement. He had been right. The jewelled cameos were connected with the royal apartments –

If so, is it one of a hoard [Magnus Faro's account continued], hidden for safe keeping? Could buried treasure be the reason for the earlier 'accidents', and is this a case of murder? Was the drowning of Connor and Doyle also murder? There is something very suspicious about that 'purloined' boat.

Have talked to Dowie. Have learned enough to be warned that I must go carefully now.

Went to see Dowie again, but was turned away. Perhaps he is already dead. These devils will have no mercy and I must protect my dear Mary and the boy.

There could be danger.

The last words were heavily underscored. Faro turned the page, but there were no more entries. Again he read that last entry. It was dated 1 August 1837.

Two days after his interview with Dowie, Constable Faro had met his death. Returning from duty in the early hours of the morning, crossing the High Street, a runaway cab had hurtled towards him, and trying to seize the horses he had been trampled to death.

The cab was never traced and the inquest recorded 'death by misadventure', with Mary Faro protesting that the verdict should be 'murder by person or persons unknown' and that her husband had been killed by someone with a grudge against him. What better reason, thought Jeremy sadly, re-reading his father's last heavily underscored words, '*There could be danger.*' What had Dowie warned him of in his dying breath that threatened Constable Faro and his entire family? As he put the notes together, he heard the clock in the hall chime four. The Police Surgeon might not release Vince for several hours.

Faro sighed. He did not count patience among his few remaining virtues and sending Mrs Brook out to summon a gig, armed with walking stick and supported on a wave of enthusiasm and excitement, he decided to begin his investigations with a visit to the royal apartments of Edinburgh Castle.

The effect of reading his father's casebook as well as the attempt on his own life on Castle Road made Faro more than usually watchful. His sixth sense warned that his home was being watched and as he awaited the arrival of the gig at the dining-room window, was it coincidence that a strange man, his face well concealed by a high collar, was apparently searching for a house number? On the rare occasions when Faro rode out with Vince, he felt uneasily that they were being followed at a discreet distance by a small carriage with blinds drawn.

He patted his greatcoat pocket containing Queen Mary's jewel. If this formed part of a treasure hoard long concealed in the walls of Edinburgh Castle, he might be dealing with desperate men anxious to get their hands on it. The presence in 9 Sheridan Place of his mother and daughters gave him added cause for anxiety. How to warn them without causing unnecessary distress? He shook his head. A tricky situation which would need urgent but careful handling.

There was only one method, a method which although hazardous had paid off in the past. Lay the bait, draw the enemy fire. As a carriage swung into the street and he limped towards the front gate, it was no shadowy watcher who erupted before his startled gaze, but the substantial shape of Constable Gregg, who, saluting smartly, indicated the vehicle.

'Superintendent Mackintosh's compliments, Inspector, and will you be so good as to present yourself at his office immediately? The Superintendent knows about you being lame at the moment, but I am to assure you that you would not be troubled unless it was a matter of the utmost urgency.'

At the Central Office, he found Superintendent Mackintosh in a less than understanding mood and dismissive of his Senior Detective Inspector's injury. His scornful manner declared more than any words that this had been caused by incompetence combined with a reckless disregard for personal safety.

'Clambering about rocks, Faro. You should leave that sort of thing to the constables. That's what we employ them for.'

Useless to murmur that they didn't always use their imagination when looking for clues.

'Imagination? What has that to do with it? We don't keep them to use their imaginations. Evidence based on solid fact and logic, that's all we pay for, all we get and indeed, all we have a right to expect,' he added self-righteously.

'Is that what you wanted to tell me, Superintendent?' asked Faro heavily.

Mackintosh made an impatient gesture. 'Of course not. Jock Clavers has been seen, in the neighbourhood of Glencorse. We have information that he has gone to earth, winged by one of the gamekeepers during the last robbery. Anyway, our informer tells us he is hiding in the folly on Lord Wylie's estate.'

'When did you hear this?'

'Just before we sent for you.'

Faro wondered who had clyped and why. If it had been one of his regulars then the Superintendent would have told him.

'It won't be dark until ten o'clock,' he continued, 'so this is an opportunity not to be missed. Clavers's daughter worked there as servant lass. Bearing in mind that his lairdship is a sheriff, I thought he might appreciate having the arrest made by someone in authority, rather than a bevy of police constables descending on him. Just in case the report is false. Don't you agree?'

At any other time, Faro would have been delighted to know that the elusive Clavers had been run to earth. Safely behind bars, the baffling six months of unsolved robberies would be at an end. All were from stately homes and bore the Clavers gang's unmistakable imprint. Jewellery, ornaments, plate, pictures and other valuable items worth several thousand pounds had been taken, and the irate owners were increasingly annoyed by the Police Force's singular lack of success in tracing the thieves and restoring their property.

'I don't need to tell you that this would be a feather in your cap, Faro, if you could nab Clavers. He's damned clever, but he's bound to make a mistake sooner or later.'

'Who is your informer?'

Mackintosh shook his head. 'The fewer who know this person's identity the better, Faro. That was part of the bargain. We've been trying to get Clavers for a long time now and all you need to know is that our informant is very much in our debt and anxious to prove reliable. Take some lads in readiness. I don't need to tell you to spread them around discreetly in case he makes a bolt for it.'

'Any word on the Edinburgh Castle break-in yet?'

'No. And I rather fancy there won't be any either. Clear as daylight that this is a case of death by misadventure. Man was climbing where he had no business to be in the first place.'

'Is there anything in the missing persons file that would identify him?'

The Superintendent sighed. 'That's the first place we looked, Faro. We've made the routine enquiries, had a couple with missing fathers, half a dozen absconding husbands, but none of them identified the corpse.' He chuckled grimly. 'Most of the wives we saw were very put out and distressed, I might tell you, that the dead man wasn't the absconded husband. Bitterly disappointed they were. You should have heard the reproaches from a couple of them, as if we had lured them to the Office on false pretences, with a guarantee of widow's weeds and the chance they had been waiting for, to enjoy the insurance.'

Picking up some papers on his desk in an attitude of dismissal, Mackintosh said, 'We'll give the corpse another week to enjoy the mortuary's cold hospitality and then we'll have him tidied away and the case closed.'

'Tidied away' was the Superintendent's delicate way of saying that the unclaimed body would be given to the Medical College for dissection.

'And if someone claims him?'

'I would imagine they'd want him underground as soon as possible. They don't keep well in this weather. Nor do

I imagine they'll want to be involved in any scandal about what he might have been doing on Castle Rock. Elderly relatives can be embarrassing, they get odd ideas.'

And as Faro rose from the chair with some effort, Mackintosh added, 'McQuinn was just going off duty. I asked him to stay. You won't be much use if it comes to a chase and he's a good man to have along with you if Clavers turns nasty or makes a bolt for it.'

Remembering that Glencorse bordered Piperlees, Faro collected the dead man's jacket and ordered a police carriage. While waiting, Faro stood at the window of his room and considered the Queen Mary cameo now reposing in his pocket in a new light.

Could it have any connection with Clavers's robberies? Had they been planning a grand *coup* on the royal apartments, and was the unknown man a member of the gang?

No. Much as the tidiness of the theory appealed to him, Faro decided that this was a case of imagination and wishful thinking gaining precedence over common sense. Years of experience had lent him an ability to recognise instantly the habitual criminal and house-breaker. Whatever had led to that clumsy attempt on the Castle Rock, the dead man's age and air of genteel poverty did not fit the pattern of Clavers's highly organised and successful gang, most of whom were under thirty-five and extremely agile.

There was only one way to make certain. Make a drawing of the jewel he had found and have the police show it at each of the houses where the robberies had taken place.

No mean draughtsman, Faro was quite pleased with his effort when a short time afterwards he emerged from his office to find McQuinn waiting impatiently.

Half an hour later, the carriage turned into the leafy drive of Lord Wylie's estate, admirably situated for concealment of the police reinforcements.

With McQuinn unhampered by a walking stick in the lead, Faro cautiously approached the folly, using the natural screen of vegetation to give as much cover as possible.

McQuinn leaped up the steps and at his touch the door flew open without the least effort. Even before he could issue his stern warning, Faro knew that they were too late.

Clavers had eluded the net once again.

With a raging, frustrated McQuinn cursing at his side, he limped back along the drive. The sustained effort of walking quickly was still painful and he was glad to take a seat in the waiting carriage.

'Seeing we have come this far,' he told McQuinn, 'we might as well continue to Piperlees and try to find out something about the jacket here while there's still light.'

A look of annoyance crossed McQuinn's face. He knew he could not refuse this extra duty much as it irked and inconvenienced him. 'I was wondering about that. Could it possibly be one of yours, I thought. A bit shabby for a Detective Inspector.' He laughed. 'But men who are getting on seem to prefer old clothes, more comfortable, they tell me . . . '

Another splendid chance of indicating that his superior was old and decrepit, thought Faro, biting back his anger and resolving to cheat McQuinn of the satisfaction of seeing him rise to the bait.

Truth to be told, Faro would have vastly preferred to have Vince with him at Piperlees, but when they were so near it seemed an opportunity not to be missed. Especially with a police carriage at their disposal, for it would be a dismal and wearying journey on his own from Edinburgh and back again in his present crippled condition.

Turning into the drive of Piperlees, Faro decided that his mission would appear more casual if he visited Sir James alone. The presence of the police could be intimidating. An almost unfailing reaction which Faro had witnessed with carefully suppressed amusement through the years. How even the most respectable and innocent of citizens were prone to display feelings of resentment, reticence and, at the pricking of uneasy conscience, even unaccountable guilt at the presence in their house of a uniformed sergeant or constable.

As the drive swept round towards the handsome mansion, lights blazed from the windows and the presence of several carriages with waiting coachmen indicated that Sir James had guests.

'Looks like a party,' said McQuinn.

Faro ignored the obvious. 'One more carriage won't matter then.'

With instructions to McQuinn to wait, he limped up to the front door, which was opened with alacrity by a manservant.

'Is Sir James at home? Detective Inspector Faro.'

The servant was unimpressed. 'What is your business?'

Faro thought hard. He could hardly present Sir James with one of his discarded jackets in the middle of dinner.

'It won't take long, just a routine enquiry.'

'Then you had better enquire again tomorrow and perhaps Sir James will see you then.'

The servant stood firm, ready to close the door. Turning to leave, cursing this lost opportunity when time was such an important factor, Faro thought quickly. If not Sir James, then there was one other person who might have the information he sought.

'Sir James's valet – I don't suppose he would be available for a word?'

The servant smirked. 'You suppose right. Mr Peters is out for the evening and I don't know when he'll return. Besides, if you have questions to ask any of the staff, you will have to seek Sir James's permission first.'

Retreating to the carriage, he was met with, 'Wouldn't see you, sir? Too bad.' McQuinn enjoyed seeing the Inspector discomfited.

'I'll see him tomorrow. And I'll be obliged if you do not mention this visit. Keep it unofficial,' Faro added, disliking intensely asking this favour and thereby putting himself under an obligation to the Sergeant.

McQuinn merely nodded, his thoughts plainly elsewhere. And so with the feelings of frustration so familiar to him in his role as detective, Faro sat back to gloomily endure the rest of the journey. If there was any satisfaction to be gained it was in bequeathing to the odious McQuinn the unenviable task of imparting to Superintendent Mackintosh that Clavers had escaped them once again.

As he left the carriage outside his home, the sun had already set in scarlet glory behind the Pentland Hills. Another day ended. Faro's conscience smote him anew. Soon his family would be returning to Orkney, leaving him full of guilt at having spent so little time with Rose and Emily. Each time they met, he was surprised to find yet another stranger child. Taller, subtly changed, escaping into girlhood, and leaving him still yearning for the wee bairns he had unaccountably lost. One day, if he wasn't very careful, he knew that he might find to his eternal regret two young women, complete strangers, asking his permission to marry and the family life he had hardly known would be ended before it had properly begun.

Stepping through his own front door, he was full of splendid resolutions. It felt good to be home, especially to have his little daughters waiting in their nightgowns to embrace him. Their well-scrubbed faces, their shining hair, their squeals of delight, indicated how much they had missed him. Here was dear Papa, the long-absent traveller returned at last. Such a welcome would have melted the hardest of hearts and Faro, who rarely shed tears, was choked with emotion as he gathered them to his heart.

Mrs Brook was there with anxious enquiries about his supper. His mother fussed as usual. He smiled wryly. For her he would never be Detective Inspector Jeremy Faro, a man of responsibility and decision, approaching middle age. For her he was just one other child.

'Now you've seen Papa home again. They were allowed to wait up for you,' said Mrs Faro. 'Do let Papa have some peace, girls. He has been working hard all day. So say good night and off to bed with you.'

'Just a little longer . . . ' whispered Emily.

'Please, Papa,' sighed Rose.

'We would love a story – please, Papa.'

'Oh yes, yes, indeed we would.'

'Then you shall have one.'

Climbing the stairs between them, holding two tiny hands in his large fists, while they accommodated their nimble steps to his awkward gait, solicitious for his poor injured ankle, Faro felt uncommonly cosseted and well blessed. The picture of doting fatherhood, he proudly settled them in the big spare-room bed.

'Now, what sort of story would you like?'

Emily pointed towards the window. 'Tell us about King Arthur.'

'Yes,' said Rose reproachfully. 'You promised you would.'

He told them how Arthur's Seat had got its name. How King Arthur and his knights fought the dog-faced warriors of the Hybee tribe on that very spot they could see where the last rays of the day's sunlight glowed red and faded into the dark. How bravely they fought for a day and a night and the sound of the battle reverberated like a thunderstorm over the surrounding countryside.

Hopelessly outnumbered, bleeding from many wounds, defeat and death seemed inevitable. But the faery kingdom was on Arthur's side. When all seemed lost, a great door appeared in the hillside and the King with his loyal knights were whisked inside. There it was promised they would live for ever. Unless a day came when their country was in dire peril from other invaders and the horn which had slipped from King Arthur's saddle was found again. Should someone blow that faery horn, then the great door would again open and the King and his knights would ride out to victory.

'Is the horn still hidden, Papa?'

'I hope no one blows it by accident,' whispered Emily, who was inclined to be nervous.

'I wonder if there are any clues as to where it might be hidden,' was the practical Rose's response. 'I shall certainly keep my eyes open, Papa. You may rely on that and I shall look for anything unusual the next time Vince takes us . . . ' Her words were lost in a sleepy yawn.

Having kissed them good night, Faro went downstairs somewhat cynically concluding that there was as much hope of Rose finding King Arthur's horn as he had of unravelling a thirty-three-year-old mystery. If it hadn't been for the coincidence of the two identical jewels he would have been almost inclined to let it stay unsolved.

The dead man's identity was vital. Dowie, if he were still alive, would be the right age. However, he had been present at Vince's examination of the body which had revealed no injury or scars to account for the 1837 report of 'serious injury' and Magnus Faro's remark 'He is far gone' surely indicated approaching death.

In a few days it would be too late, anyhow. Corpses couldn't be kept indefinitely and once the body was disposed of to the Medical School, Faro could not imagine Superintendent Mackintosh allowing him to waste his time on an investigation based on purely nebulous speculation. The Superintendent was a tidy man and he would be keen to have the case closed and the unknown Castle Rock victim would become just one more mysterious death in Edinburgh's turbulent history.

Lost, unsolved, for ever.

Chapter Six

At ten o'clock next morning, Faro limped across the Castle quadrangle only to be told that his journey had been in vain.

'Sir Eric has been summoned to Balmoral Castle – by HM,' said the young officer, adding 'Her Majesty', apologetically, in case the jargon of officialdom was unknown to a Detective Inspector.

'Mr Forster, Sir Eric's personal assistant, is unable to be here. I have been left in charge: Lieutenant Arthur Mace,' he said by way of introduction. Then solemnly consulting a list: 'Yes, Inspector, you are expected. Sir Eric states that you are to examine the royal apartments in connection with the recent attempted break in.'

Over the short distance to their destination, Faro observed his companion carefully. The smart new uniform somewhat self-consciously worn suggested that he was new to responsibility and to the regiment of Scots Greys. Faro would have hazarded a guess that the lad was little past twenty, and his upper-class English accent indicated that after leaving public school his family had bought him a commission.

Unlocking the door, Mace turned. 'Sir Eric said I was to assure you that since your last meeting he had instructed Mr Forster to make a most careful search and Mr Forster was satisfied that nothing had been disturbed in the attempted burglary.'

Walking round the glass cases, Faro merely nodded. There was no evidence of locks being forced and a brief examination of the windows was enough to confirm the assistant keeper's report.

Faro cursed silently. The trail, if any had existed, was already cold.

'I have always been absolutely fascinated by Mary Queen of Scots,' said Mace with a sigh. 'Look at that dear little shoe of hers and the glove. Such tiny feet and hands and I'm told that she was six foot tall. Tall, indeed, for a man in those days.'

'Or for anyone, if the height of doorways is to be believed.'

Mace opened the door into the Queen's bedchamber and sighed again. 'I wish I had lived then.'

Faro looked at Mace's high forehead, his long pale face and long slender hands. Quite remarkable. Mace might have stepped down from a portrait of that period and he smiled in sympathy.

'A savage, cruel time, it was.'

'But there was beauty, such chivalry, don't you think, dying for a young and beautiful Queen.'

Faro said nothing. The lad was half in love with a ghost, as he himself had once been. Let him keep his illusions. Romantic young fools like this one had gone to bloody death in their dozens, by way of the torture chamber and the block, their lofty ideals and sufferings vanished into the dust of passing centuries. Of that tragic long-ago only a few pathetic faded artefacts remained, objects which might, or might not, have once belonged to the Queen. He touched the bed curtains reputed to have been embroidered during her long years of imprisonment. What secrets, what thoughts of agony and grief had she woven into those delicate patterns which had alone remained impervious to time?

'Isn't our present Queen the one you would gladly die for,' Faro asked, 'seeing that you have taken her shilling?'

Mace looked confused and embarrassed. 'Yes, I suppose so. Of course,' he added, but without any true conviction.

Faro smiled. The poor lad's heart wasn't in it, to die for the royal widow, whose preoccupation with mourning Prince Albert, unpopular and misunderstood by the masses, suggested neglect of important matters of government, as well as the rumoured neglect of her subjects. A Queen who, stout after much child bearing, could only command her generation of romantic young fools to die on the battle-field of yet another outpost of her ever-growing Empire, hard won and even harder to hold.

Mace pushed open the door of the tiny room high above the Castle Rock. In area it was not much larger than a linen closet in Sheridan Place, yet here Queen Mary had given birth to the future King James VI of Scotland and I of England.

Here, as in no other room in the Castle associated with the Queen, Faro was conscious of a lingering sense of dis-aster and doom well beyond a monarch's personal tragedy. Here, from these very stones, emanated the events that had reverberated through Scotland's subsequent history, when a once-powerful nation took the wrong turning to wither and die from the effects of Jacobitism and the Clearances.

Standing by the window, he was engulfed by a miasma of foreboding. Distorted whispers, faint cries echoed around him, as if only a thin veil divided the long-ago from now. He closed his eyes, seeking desperately to renew his own link with that time, half remembered, hovering on the brink of what his mother called 'long memory': their Stuart blood, via the Orkney Sinclairs and the Wicked Earl, an explana-tion too fanciful for her son's fierce logic to accept.

Again Faro considered the steep slope of Castle Rock. Inaccessible from inside or outside the barred window, he concluded that no man in his right senses would have the folly or initiative to attempt its scaling. He would have given much to have known how the dead man had spent his last hour.

Mace locked the doors behind them. 'Is there anything else I can do for you, Inspector, any information I can help you with?'

It was a forlorn hope, but Faro produced the two cameos. 'Have you ever seen these before?'

Mace studied the jewels carefully. 'No, I haven't, I regret to say. But I am almost certain these miniatures are of Queen Mary and Darnley, possibly at the time of their marriage.' His voice increased in excitement as he continued, 'May I ask how you came by them, Inspector?'

'They came into my possession recently.' Faro was not prepared to say more that that.

'Are they from a collection?' Mace asked eagerly.

'Perhaps so. I know little of their history. I was hoping they might have come from the royal apartments.'

'Stolen, you mean?' Mace sounded profoundly shocked.

'Yes, that is why I am here, to discover if any items are missing.'

Mace smiled sadly. 'I wish they were mine. You see, my family has a great many trinkets of this period, and I would be willing to swear that these pieces are authentic.' He nodded enthusiastically. 'Yes, indeed, you can take my word for it. These are more likely to have been the personal possessions of Queen Mary than most of the artefacts in the Castle.' He paused. 'If you have a moment, Inspector, I should like to check the inventory of the Queen's jewels.'

Mace walked quickly across the quadrangle and unlocked a room containing narrow stacks of dusty files. He pointed across to dismembered suits of armour, swords and pistols, heaped together with a rusty 'iron maiden' off its supports.

'These are awaiting reconstruction, for exhibition in the new museum. I am something of an expert in this kind of work. A labour of love, one might say,' continued Mace happily.

Faro declined the invitation for a closer inspection and took the opportunity to rest his ankle. A much frayed and dilapidated velvet chair, upon whose interior he suspected rats had freely feasted, did not deter him. He sat down and a few moments later Mace emerged from the labyrinth triumphantly clutching a roll of yellowed documents.

'This inventory of the Queen's jewels is absolutely fascinating and quite unique. Much of it dates from the time of her reign, written by her Lord Chamberlain. Later we have documents from the time of her first imprisonment at Lochleven and later in England when her possessions were being listed by her jailers at the request of Queen Elizabeth. The miniatures should date these two pieces fairly accurately. Most likely painted and exchanged at the time of their betrothal early in 1565 and certainly not later than Darnley's murder at Kirk o'Field in 1567.'

'So short a time,' said Faro. 'Presumably they were disposed of immediately after she married the Earl of Bothwell.'

Mace nodded, rifling through the parchments. 'Indeed, in the circumstances, it's highly unlikely that the Queen would wish to keep any mementoes of her second husband.' Mace paused and looked across at Faro. 'How very strange. The inventory of the jewels. It isn't here in its usual place. Quite extraordinary.' He shrugged. 'Perhaps it is away being catalogued. Yes, that would be the answer. I'm sorry to disappoint you, Inspector. Mr Forster will know. I'll find out from him and let you know.'

'If you would be so kind, a note to the Central Office will find me.'

'Very well. And now, how else can I help you?'

'I'm not sure. You are very knowledgeable about Queen Mary.'

Mace beamed. 'History is my speciality. My own family dates from the sixteenth century. Such a time to live, so rich in romance.'

'And in mayhem and murder,' said Faro, a suggestion which Mace chose to ignore. 'Do you happen to know anything of a child's remains allegedly discovered hidden in the wall of the royal apartments?'

'Oh, that fairy tale.' Mace laughed. 'We know now that it was a practical joke.'

'Surely someone with a rather macabre sense of humour?'

'It was the idea of the officers of the guard apparently, to frighten the workmen repairing the wall.'

'I dare say they succeeded,' Faro remarked drily. 'To be frank with you, a child's body doesn't sound like a practical joke in the best of good taste.'

'But to the uneducated labouring class, Inspector? Take the bones of some small animal, most likely a monkey, wrap them in an old vestment. Tell them these are the mummified remains of a child interred long ago and such information, from their superiors, would be accepted without the least question. Surely you can imagine, Inspector, how irresistible such a prank would seem to young, high-spirited army officers. One knows how gullible Irish workmen are,' Mace giggled, with a touch of malice.

Faro eyed him with sudden distaste. 'A highly reputable newspaper – the *Scotsman* – also accepted the discovery as fact and, indeed, reported it in considerable detail.'

'Come now, Inspector, we are all aware that news reports are prone to exaggeration,' said Mace with a pitying smile. 'Sensational stories are what they rely upon to sell their newspapers. And I don't imagine, for one moment, that the writer was encouraged to examine the contents of the coffin in case he realised that these were not, in fact, the bones of a child at all.'

'Not any child, Lieutenant. The remains were rumoured to be those of a royal prince, the son Queen Mary bore to Darnley.'

Again Mace laughed. 'No scholar would take such a preposterous supposition seriously, Inspector. You are surely not suggesting that King James VI of Scotland and Queen Elizabeth's legitimate successor was an impostor?'

Faro smiled. 'You know, I really hadn't got that far. But now that you mention it, yes, perhaps we have a point worthy of consideration.'

Mace looked nonplussed. 'If this were true, Inspector, then a lot of history would have to be rewritten. And I can assure you that no loyal servant of HM would ever harbour such treasonable and sinister thoughts,' he added severely.

Faro nodded. 'The Castle officials made absolutely certain that no one else would have any opportunity to investigate. The remains were immediately re-interred and the aperture sealed.' He took advantage of the Lieutenant's sudden bewildered expression to add sharply, 'Have you any idea why Colonel Lazenby committed suicide in 1837, at the time of the second discovery?'

'I gather he was involved in some scandal.' Mace's tone expressed contempt and disapproval. 'Why do you ask?'

'As he was in charge of the Castle restorations, I just wondered if there might be some possible connection.'

Mace laughed out loud. 'Good heavens, Inspector, it was nothing to do with a practical joke on some ignorant workmen that drove Lazenby to such dire straits.'

'You think falling off a scaffolding was a practical joke?'

'Of course not, Inspector.' Mace's countenance flushed red with indignation as he added stiffly, 'You are deliberately misunderstanding me. I was referring to our earlier discussion.'

'What about Lazenby then?'

'I understand it was a sordid matter, hushed up by the regiment. Lazenby was involved with a married woman, the wife of a fellow officer. Disgrace to his colours . . . '

'Oh indeed,' Faro interrupted. 'I understood from his obituary that he had been recently married.'

Mace had recovered. He raised one eyebrow mockingly. 'Since when, Inspector, did such peccadillos influence a man's reasons for making a suitable marriage? When he was challenged by the woman's husband, suicide was the only decent thing left to him to avoid a scandal.' He stood up. 'And now, is there anything else I can do for you?'

Faro sensed by the way he gathered his papers together that Mace's co-operation had been replaced by a somewhat chilly impatience.

'There is one more thing, Lieutenant. My history book contains only one chapter on Queen Mary's reign. I wonder if you have a more comprehensive volume in your library.'

Mace seemed relieved by the request, his good humour restored. 'Of course, Inspector. Over here.' He went to the shelves. 'An excellent account based on contemporary records. The only copy in existence. It's very valuable and I'm afraid it cannot be removed from the building. However, you may consult it here at your leisure.'

Seeing the Inspector settled at a table by the window, Mace shook hands, wished him good day, saying what a pleasure it had been, and promising to be in communication as soon as Mr Forster revealed the present whereabouts of the missing inventory.

Through a regular study of lengthy documents, Faro had acquired of necessity an ability to read fast. He also possessed a remarkable visual memory and, although the prose of the book was stiff and awesome to a modern reader, he knew exactly what he was looking for.

Two hours later, he heard the one o'clock gun fired from the battlements. Armed with copious notes copied from the volume, he was leaving the building when he caught a glimpse of Lucille Haston alighting from a carriage in the quadrangle outside Sir Eric's apartments. As he drew nearer, he saw that she was in the process of upbraiding her maid.

'And stop being so sullen – remember you're getting all my old clothes, so do try to look happy and grateful for once.' Catching sight of the Inspector, Lucille giggled apologetically. 'I am quite exhausted. So much shopping.'

'So I see.' And Faro limped forward gallantly to offer the dour Bet a sympathetic hand as she staggered out of the carriage buried in an assortment of boxes bearing the names of Edinburgh's mantle and millinery shops.

'For heaven's sake, she can manage,' said Lucille, watching him indignantly. 'Men look so ridiculous carrying hat boxes.'

'It seems that you find our shops to your taste,' he said.

'I do indeed. Such rapturous clothes. Quite on a par with London and Paris fashions, I understand. Uncle Eric is away to Balmoral Castle, if you please. At the command of Her Majesty, who didn't see fit to invite his poor niece.'

Bet opened the door for her mistress and as Faro deposited the two large boxes in her charge, Lucille removed her bonnet, fluffed out her hair and sighed. 'Really, Inspector, it is too bad. Here I am positively dying of boredom. If only one had friends of one's own age, it would be bearable.'

And, he thought, regarding him very intently, she added, 'I'm starved. Have you had luncheon? No? Good. Then Bet will find us something.'

'Thank you, but I'm afraid you must excuse me. I am expected home to Sheridan Place. My daughters . . . ' he ended somewhat lamely.

'Oh, I had forgotten. The two little girls.' And wistfully, 'Tell me their names again.'

'Rose and Emily.'

'Rose and Emily,' she repeated slowly. 'I would so love to meet them. I wonder – I wonder, if I might take them to the Botanic Gardens this afternoon. I have the carriage at my disposal.' And laying a hand on his arm, she said, 'Please say yes, I really am quite desperate for company and I have no idea how long Uncle Eric will be absent.'

There was, Faro knew, only one answer. 'Then permit me to invite you to luncheon with us. I am sure Rose and Emily – and my mother – will be delighted to receive you.'

Lucille clasped her hands, jumping up and down with excitement and truth to tell, he thought, looked so ingenuous and charming that she seemed little older than his own daughters at that moment.

'Oh, do you mean it? Really? Oh, I would so love that. Such paradise. I can't tell you how this dreary old Castle gets on my nerves. It isn't a bit as I imagined it. Artists always make it look so romantic – and I suppose it is on the outside. But inside, its exactly like living in a barracks. I so long for female society.' And indicating the carriage. 'Shall we go?'

'Hadn't you better tell your maid?'

She frowned. 'Oh yes, I suppose so. But you had better come with me. Tell her that you are an old and trusted friend of Uncle Eric, and so on.'

Confronted by the stony-faced Bet, Faro was astonished at his young companion's elaborations. Not only was he a family friend of Sir Eric, and a policeman, but Uncle Eric had especially entrusted her into his keeping while he was visiting the Queen.

At the end of this glowing testimony, with only the vaguest indication of when to expect her return, Lucille hurried him out of the door, down the stone steps and into Sir Eric's private carriage, which he soon discovered was a vast improvement on the police vehicle in the matter of interior furnishings. As they trotted briskly down the High Street he was amazed to find that the well-upholstered red plush seats with their buttoned padded backs left passengers quite impervious to the normal jolts and discomfort of travelling over the cobbles.

All the way to Sheridan Place, hardly stopping to draw breath, Lucille prattled happily on a vast assortment of topics, with such speed and diversity that Faro soon lost the thread.

He felt his concentration glazing over, but soon discovered that his silence went unnoticed. A pleasant smile, a nod of approval and an interested expression were enough. When Lucille asked a question she never waited for nor, he suspected, did she even expect an answer.

Handing her down from the carriage and opening his front door, he tried not to observe that his mother's jaw had dropped open at the sight of the pretty young girl at her son's side. A look that was swiftly replaced, he noted with some amusement, by one he knew well. His mother was already hearing the distant chime of wedding bells.

Nor was his mother alone. The same thoughts were obviously running through Mrs Brook's mind.

'No, Inspector sir, of course I can lay another place for luncheon. No, it isn't in the least inconvenient,' she added to his whispered aside. 'Delighted, I'm sure.' The latter was accompanied by an approving though markedly sly look in Lucille's direction.

By the time luncheon was at an end. Mary Faro had summed up Lucille Haston. She had all her case history and was clearly weighing the evidence. Was this a just case for a verdict of marriage? What an admirable detective his mother would have made, thought Faro.

On the other side of the table, Rose and Emily, with Lucille between them, chatted happily.

'Just look at that, son,' said Mary Faro. 'How they've taken to Miss Haston. Why, anyone would think they had known her all their lives,' she added in a tone laden with significance, as the two little girls were sent upstairs to wash hands and faces before the promised outing to the Botanic Gardens.

'You must come too, Miss Haston,' said Emily.

'Yes, Papa has an inside closet, you must use it,' said Rose, always practical.

'Girls – really,' said Mrs Faro in a shocked voice. 'We don't boast about such things.'

Lucille beamed upon her. 'I'm delighted by the information, Mrs Faro. We haven't anything so modern in the backwoods where I come from.'

Faro was waiting when they came downstairs. 'May I beg a lift in your splendid carriage as far as the High Street?'

'Delighted, I'm sure.'

He sat between Rose and Emily, who held his hands with a distinct air of possession and occasionally leaned over to kiss his cheek while Miss Haston, seated opposite, gave him her undivided attention. The glances in his direction were so unmistakably admiring that Faro felt idiotically happy, out of all proportion to the occasion.

'Why do you smile, Papa?' asked the observant Rose.

'I was just thinking that this is a perfect day for a visit to the Botanic Gardens. I do envy you.'

'Come with us, Papa.'

'Yes, please, Papa.'

'Such a waste to remain indoors on a beautiful day,' was Lucille's reproachful comment.

Faro shook his head. Criminals did not cease from crime because of fine summer weather.

'How lovely the hills look, all shimmering and mysterious,' Lucille continued, opening the window so that a pleasant breeze wafted into the carriage. 'They remind me so of home – I must go there and walk one day before I leave.'

Faro was tempted to make the offer which he felt that this remark with its accompanying glance blatantly invited. However, he remembered that other occasion not so very long ago when he had taken pity on a lonely lady, a stranger to Edinburgh, and how their first excursion together had been to the Pentlands. To think how that had ended . . .

No. He must not remember. He had trained himself in forgetfulness and he would not allow Miss Haston to open that storehouse of bitter memories.

As he left them in the High Street, his daughters bestowed their ritual of smacking kisses while Miss Haston watched wistfully, as if she would have liked to be included.

Faro felt quite confused as he walked towards the Central Office. Perhaps he had hurt her feelings, perhaps he should have kissed her gently and innocently on the cheek, indicating that he regarded her in the same light as Rose and Emily. To kiss or not to kiss. Oh dear, what was a man to do?

Once inside his office, all such domestic problems were instantly forgotten. His presence was being eagerly sought by the Superintendent, who had just been alerted to yet another hiding place of the elusive Clavers, recently sighted at Leith.

The police carriage with its reinforcement of constables set out at a brisk pace for the harbour. They were too late. There was no evidence of Clavers and his gang in the now deserted shipping warehouse where they had allegedly gone to earth.

At this stage, Faro began to have serious doubts as to the integrity of the Superintendent's informant. He had a strong suspicion that his superior officer was being extremely gullible, deliberately misled by one of the gang or even one of Clavers's doxies (of which he was reported to have a considerable number, along with a remarkable capacity for keeping them all happy).

Retracing his steps to the police carriage waiting in the shade offered by the nearby church for the hot dusty ride back into Edinburgh, he read, 'St Patrick's Roman Catholic Church. Reverend Father James O'Rourke.'

Faro remembered his father's casebook. The John Femister who had died in 1837 had been from Leith. His fellow labourers were believed to be from Ireland in which case they were most likely Catholics. So there was always the remote possibility that they might have been interred in the one burial ground of that denomination in Leith.

Instructing the driver to wait, he wandered round the kirkyard inspecting the graves. As the church bore the date '1820' carved in stone, most of them were relatively modern.

There was no Matthew O'Hara or Peter Dowie and he was ready to give up when he came upon a headstone half-hidden by weeds, 'Jean Femister, died 1832, aged 29 years, beloved wife of John Femister, died 1837 aged 35 years. R.I.P.'

Returning once more to the grave of the sadly young couple, he suddenly realised the significance of its neglect. The Femisters had left no close and caring relatives. Yet, according to the newspaper, Femister had left a daughter. Was she the reason for her mother's early death? He did a rapid calculation. She would be about his own age, and with luck, she might have survived.

There was one way to find out. He set off along the gravel path leading to the church, where his further investigations were thwarted by a locked door. Disconsolately, he walked around the building and was about to leave when a priest hurried across the grass, his eager expression suggesting that Faro's attention to the gravestones had not gone unnoticed.

'Is there someone in particular you are seeking, sir?'

As Faro explained, his hopes of success faded. This rosy-faced cherubic priest was considerably less than forty.

'Alas, I cannot help you. I am new to this area. Father Bruce would have known. He was here for fifty years.'

'Perhaps I could talk to him?'

The priest shook his head and pointed solemnly to a new grave with a shining monument of a hovering angel. 'There he lies, sir. Buried three months past. Your best hope now is the parish records. If you'll come with me.'

Inside five minutes Faro had all the information he needed: John Femister's marriage in 1831 and a year later, the birth of a daughter, Griselda, and the death of his wife, Jean.

He found Father O'Rourke in the dim, cool interior with its odours of incense and the smell of old Bibles peculiar to stone-walled churches.

'Griselda Femister? No, I am certain there is no one of that name in our congregation. If she was only five when her father died then it is most likely that relatives took care of her – if she had any.'

And perhaps took her many miles from Leith. Without knowing their names it would be a hopeless task to trace her. Besides a child of five might have only the vaguest memories of her father and remember even less about the circumstances surrounding his death.

'If she had no relatives,' the priest continued, 'then she would have been placed in one of our orphanages, either in Edinburgh or in the Lothians. However, if she remained in the district and eventually married, then of course, she would most likely have been married at our church.' And when Faro looked hopeful, 'Perhaps you would like to consult the marriage register?'

Back in the vestry, Faro ignored all entries before 1848 as it was unlikely that Griselda Femister would have married before she was sixteen. It was not until March 1853 that he found the entry he sought, 'Griselda Femister, daughter of the late John and Jean Femister of this parish, and Malcolm Penfold, baron, of Heriot Row, Edinburgh.' Neither of the witnesses, alas, were Femisters.

Lord Penfold was well known to every member of the Edinburgh City Police. A High Court judge, a respected member of Edinburgh society, he was also a pillar of the Church of Scotland. What of his wife? Had she changed her religion?

Thanking the young priest, Faro made his way back to the police carriage, eminently satisfied with his afternoon's work and delighted by the discovery of a lead, however tenuous, to those events of 1837.

There was always the chance that Lady Penfold might produce foster parents, relatives or friends with long memories. And it was by painstakingly following such minor clues that a detective whose character was strong in patience and persistence might discover a path through the labyrinth. At the end of it, such a man might be rewarded by the revelation of many long forgotten – and often dangerous – secrets.

Chapter Seven

Faro returned home to find Vince alone in the drawing room studying Magnus Faro's notes.

'Fascinating stuff, Stepfather.'

'Where's the family?'

'Long past their bedtime. Haven't you noticed the time?'

'Did they enjoy the Botanic Gardens?'

'Positively wild with delight. By the way, I had a tantalisingly brief meeting with the delectable Miss Haston as she was leaving.'

'Did she stay to supper?'

'She did indeed. After putting the girls to bed and reading them a story. Even then she was disposed to linger. Anxiously enquiring for your welfare. Did they always keep such late hours at the Central Office?'

With a teasing glance, Vince added, 'You know, I had the distinct feeling she was most reluctant to take her departure before you returned. Wished to thank you for – I quote – introducing her to two such delightful little girls. Tell him I have had a marvellous time and that, with Mrs Faro's permission, I shall call on them tomorrow.'

And clearing his throat gently, Vince said, 'I think, seeing this is my day off, that I shall make myself quite indispensable.'

'You will enjoy riding in Sir Eric's splendid carriage.'

'That is not all I hope to enjoy, Stepfather.'

'Then I wish you joy of the lady, but do bear in mind that she is Sir Eric's niece.'

'And what do you mean by that?'

'You know what I mean, Vince lad. She is not to be regarded as one of your easy young women.'

'Easy young women? Somehow I didn't get the impression that she would be difficult or inexperienced in the ways of the world.'

'Come now, Vince, if you are intending to make a conquest...'

'A conquest, Stepfather? Seduce that delightful creature? Nothing is further from my mind.'

'So be it. If any harm comes to her while she is under my roof, you'll have me – and Sir Eric, who is even more formidable – to answer to.'

'You are losing your sense of humour, Stepfather. Or could it be that you have a fancy for the lady yourself?'

'You talk nonsense.' And irritably shrugging off the hand Vince had placed on his arm, he added, 'If I had, then I should certainly not have missed an opportunity of spending a pleasant summer afternoon in the Botanic Gardens.'

Seeing Vince's puzzlement at his rather violent response, he sighed apologetically. 'I've seen them many a time, lad, that you know, in peace and in the pursuit of criminals...'

'But not, I imagine, with anyone as adorable as Miss Haston.'

'Who is young enough to be my daughter.'

'When did that deter any lusty male? God created men to love for ever.'

'Then let me put it another way. Do you think I'll ever fall in love, after what I have been through – or have you forgotten?'

And seeing his expression, Vince patted his shoulder. 'No. And never will,' he added gently. 'Forgive me, Stepfather, I am being crass and more tactless than usual. I realise it's early days for you – after ...'

'Yes, yes,' Faro interrupted. He could not bear to go into the agonising details of his recent loss. 'And now, let's get down to these notes you've been reading.'

As he ate Mrs Brook's standard 'cold collation' left for either the doctor or the Inspector if they were unfortunate enough to miss supper, Faro filled in the details of his visit to Edinburgh Castle and his meeting with Lieutenant Arthur Mace. As he spoke, he spread the two Queen Mary jewels side by side on the small table before them.

'What do you make of it all, lad?'

Vince sat back in his chair. 'I should say, Stepfather, that, regardless of Mace's theory, whatever that tomb in the wall contained – and I'm inclined towards a treasure hoard personally – we can certainly dismiss any notion that the small coffin was a hoax and contained the remains of some small animal.'

'They couldn't have made a mistake?'

Vince shook his head. 'You don't have to be a medical man to know about such things. You couldn't mistake a mummified monkey for a child, could you?'

Faro shook his head. 'I don't think so.'

'Nor, I assure you, could the most ignorant of workmen, unless they were also half blind, which I doubt. And having read your father's notes, I am convinced that this discovery was no practical joke, but one to be taken very seriously indeed.' Pausing, he put the tips of his fingers together and regarded his stepfather thoughtfully. 'Has it not occurred to you that the existence of this small coffin hidden for nearly three hundred years might well pose one of history's most intriguing questions? Was the man who succeeded Mary as King of Scotland and England really her son or was he an impostor?'

'Yes, and in the words of Lieutenant Mace, if that were so, a great deal of our history would have to be rewritten, especially in regard to the royal succession,' Faro added slowly.

'If the baby was James, then what have we in support of our theory? Where does the secret of that tiny coffin begin?'

'Has your history improved, lad?'

Vince grinned. 'Not much. It was always my weakest

subject. Too dry and dusty when there were so many urgent matters in the present to engage one's interest. However, no one living in Edinburgh could be immune to Scotland's tragic Queen.'

'You recall David Rizzio's murder?'

'I do indeed. Every schoolboy worth his salt has gloated over the bloodstained boards in the Queen's supper room at Holyrood. Do you think it still gets another dose of ox's blood from time to time to keep it fresh?'

Faro sighed. Keeping his stepson's mind on historical facts had always been difficult. 'Doesn't it intrigue you as a medical man to wonder why the Queen, who was six months pregnant when she witnessed Rizzio murdered before her eyes, with Ruthven's sword point at her stomach, did not miscarry?'

Vince nodded. 'Wasn't her husband Darnley in the plot too?'

'He was indeed. Listen to this. It's a contemporary account from a volume in the Records Office – very forthright in its language. The Queen's Secretary, Maitland of Lethington, is reported as saying of Darnley, "He misuses himself so far towards her that it is an heartbreak for her to think that he should be her husband." Yet when he had smallpox in Glasgow she went to nurse him personally.'

'Poor Mary. Reading between the lines that smallpox was a polite name for another pox – syphilis, in fact,' said Vince.

'What an appalling discovery for any young bride – especially the Queen of Scots,' said Faro.

Vince smiled grimly. 'A discovery, alas, none too rare even in our own respectable society here in Edinburgh, if truth be told. Too much sowing of the wild oats down Leith Walk can leave a very nasty souvenir.'

'Aye, and there's a suspicion that ladies of easy virtue were not Darnley's only debaucheries.'

'A penchant for page boys?'

'Indeed. Mary must have been horrified and disgusted when so soon after marriage she discovered that her golden lad was perverted. Perhaps even worse was to know that his love for her – if it ever existed outside her imagination – came a very poor second to his lust for the throne of Scotland.'

'Let's go back to Rizzio's murder,' said Vince. 'I seem to remember the hint was that Mary and Rizzio were lovers. Do you think there was any truth in it?'

Faro snorted indignantly. 'I most certainly do not. An old grizzled hunchback. His intellect and talent as a musician must have excited and entertained her, but certainly would not be calculated to arouse her carnal appetite. From all accounts, we know that Mary was a very fastidious woman.'

'So Darnley used Rizzio as an excuse?'

'An excuse indeed. It was the throne of Scotland that Darnley was after and Mary carried the unborn heir who could displace him. He and the other conspirators were hoping that the Queen would not only miscarry but might also die and they would be rewarded for their efforts by the new King of Scots.'

'They must have planned it very carefully, especially as her health was always problematic,' said Vince. 'Sixteenth-century medicine was based on a few simple premises. Doctors believed that the human body was governed by four cardinal humours – blood, phlegm, choler and melancholy, also known as black melancholy, and it was their abundance or absence which determined a person's temperament.'

In his best textbook manner, Vince continued, 'We now know that Mary had all the symptoms of porphyria, attacks of severe abdominal pain, vomiting and diarrhoea, sometimes accompanied by a complete mental breakdown. These attacks are very severe but not long lasting and there are many women who have chronic illnesses but lose all such symptoms during pregnancy and are remarkably fit and well. And Mary must have been one such case to have survived.'

'She not only survived, lad, she used her woman's wiles.

Still wearing her gown soaked with Rizzio's blood, she persuaded Darnley she still loved him and, insisting that the conspirators meant to kill him too, she got him to help her escape from the royal apartments and flee to Dunbar, riding pillion behind one of her servants. Once she begged Darnley to slacken pace for the child's sake. "Ride on," he told her. "We can always make another bairn." God, how that thought must have revolted her.'

'What happened at Dunbar?' asked Vince.

'She was rescued by the loyal Provost of Edinburgh and the citizens and returned to the fortress of Edinburgh Castle, safer although a lot less comfortable than Holyrood, to await the birth of her child.'

'In those days, Stepfather, it was the usual custom for noble ladies to ceremoniously take to their lying-in chamber a few weeks before the birth was due and to remain there like Indian ladies in purdah.'

'What rumours there must have been down below the Castle in Edinburgh as the folk looked up wondering what on earth was taking place within its grim walls.'

'And with good reason,' said Vince. 'A husband riddled with syphilis when the child was conceived. An expectant mother who had witnessed Rizzio stabbed forty times, and her own life threatened by the murderers. Then forced to endure a twenty-five mile gallop to Dunbar – about five hours, riding pillion. Well, Stepfather, even in these civilised days, I wouldn't give much for the chances of delivering a normal child with such a prenatal background.'

'Aye, and in a less enlightened age, everyone expected her to give birth to a monster. Certainly no one expected her to leave her bed alive,' Faro added grimly.

'How did they pass the time in all those weeks of waiting?'

'The usual womanly pursuits, I imagine. Baby clothes, reading and playing the lute – and playing cards.'

'With plenty of time to make plans.'

Faro smiled. 'You are absolutely right, of course. Can't you just see them whispering together, while the Queen slept. If there was ever an opportunity, then this was when the Queen's ladies must have decided that whatever happened, on no account should Darnley rule over Scotland.'

'And if the Queen died, or the child was still-born, then a substitute royal Prince should be found. Were the four Marys still with her?'

'Only Mary Beaton, married to Ogilvie of Boyne, and niece to Margaret Forbes, Lady Reres, also in attendance. And Mary Fleming's sister was there, too – the Countess of Atholl, reputed to be a witch.'

'A loyal but strange collection of ladies, don't you think?'

'And two of them related to the original four Marys,' said Faro. 'Her oldest, dearest childhood friends. Any one of them would have died for her.'

'The perfect material for a conspiracy.'

'Let's look at Lady Reres, who was somewhat significantly, in the light of later events, also pregnant. The story of those days before the Queen was delivered . . . '

'The details of that historic royal *accouchement*, which every Scottish medical student hears about at some time,' Vince interrupted. 'It is one of the few sixteenth-century examples to be documented. A long and difficult labour . . . '

'"With the Queen so handled that she began to wish that she had never been married",' read Faro from his notes, '"and those who attended her feared for her life and the Countess of Atholl cast the childbirth pains on Lady Reres, who lay suffering with her mistress."'

'Now that is an extremely interesting coincidence. Both the Queen and Lady Reres, not only pregnant, but in childbed at the same time.'

'Was it a coincidence, or had this been carefully taken into account in the conspiracy? Remember the blood royal. Lady Reres's niece, Lady Jean Stuart, was the natural daughter of James V.'

'Mary's half-sister.'

'"When at last the Queen's sufferings were at an end, the child was born with a thin membrane over its face."'

85

'No mention of its sex – a Prince or Princess?'

'Nothing. On 19 June, it was announced that a royal Prince had been born whom Mary proclaimed her heir. But the child was not shown immediately to the waiting populace as was the custom. Even the doctors who one imagines would be in attendance maintained what might be called a stout silence. Not one word or comment on its condition.'

Vince whistled. 'In fact the doctors behaved like very loyal and cautious men.'

'Or very frightened ones. And the first time young James appears is some hours after his birth, when he is shown to Darnley. Here's the scene in the Queen's bedchamber as described by Lord Herries. "About two o'clock in the afternoon, the King came to visit the Queen and was desirous to see the child. "My Lord," says the Queen, "God has given you and me a son begotten by none but you." Then she took the child in her arms, and discovering his face said . . . "

'"Discovering his face?"' interrupted Vince. 'Did Herries mean "un-covering"?'

'I agree it is an odd expression. Does it give you the feeling that Darnley came reluctantly and wasn't offered a close look?'

'All newborn babies look alike. I should think, however, that they would want him to keep at a safe distance in his diseased condition.'

'Very convenient for our conspirators. I imagine they laid great stress upon Darnley's unwholesome presence at his wife's childbed.'

'Exactly. Proceed . . . '

'Here are Mary's words. "My Lord, here I protest to God, as I shall answer for him at the great day of Judgement, this is your own son, and no other man's son, and, as I am desirous that all here, both ladies and others, bear witness, for he is so much your own son that I fear it may be the worse for him hereafter."'

Faro laid aside the notes and waited for Vince's comments.

'Rather unusual, wouldn't you say, Stepfather?'

'"Methinks the lady doth protest too much", as the Bard would have it,' said Faro grimly.

'And there's more than a hint of warning in such an extraordinary public statement, "begotten by none but you". Suggests that Lord Darnley had been casting doubts upon the child's paternity.'

Faro consulted his notes. 'The next visitor, eight days later, was Killigrew, Ambassador of Queen Elizabeth, who reported, "I was brought to the Queen's bedside where her Highness received thankfully her Majesty's letters and commendation ..."'

Laying aside the papers, Faro smiled grimly. 'Rumour had it that Elizabeth received the glad tidings of her cousin's safe delivery by screaming, "Alack, the Queen of Scots is lighter of a bonny son, and I am but of barren stock." But to continue. Killigrew remarked upon the Queen's "delicate condition and she spoke with a hollow cough. I took leave and was brought to the young Prince sucking of his nurse."'

'Lady Reres?'

'The same.'

'How very convenient. Do go on.'

'Killigrew continued, "Afterwards I saw him as good as naked, well proportioned and like to prove a goodly prince."'

'A moment, Stepfather. Let's consider that very convenient spell of the Countess of Atholl. Since Lady Reres was wet nurse, she must have given birth recently, either immediately before or after the Queen was delivered. And if we are considering a changeling, then Lady Reres appears to be the likeliest person to provide a substitute Prince.'

'Especially as it was announced that she was to be *governante*, a kind of foster mother to the boy while the Queen was absent from Edinburgh.' Faro paused before addding, 'There is one other contender, however – the Countess of Mar. Young James was brought up in her household and I'm told that his portrait bears an uncanny resemblance to his foster brother the Second Earl of Mar, who was six years older. It is quite possible that the Countess also had another son at the same time as the Queen, and because she was related to the Lennox Stuarts she might have been persuaded to substitute her own child.'

'Which would account for that mysterious rumour which has persisted through the centuries of an infant being lowered in a basket from Edinburgh Castle. In this case, it would be the other way round,' said Vince.

'These were desperate times, lad. Loyalty was a gamble and it was all too easy to choose the wrong side. What if Mary died childless and Scotland fell into the hands of Lord Darnley and the power-crazed Lennox family? I dare say there were many frightened nobles who had a lot to lose, including ancient lands and titles, aye, and their heads, too. The only hope of peace was for Mary to leave a legitimate heir.'

'To have told Mary the truth that her agony was all in vain and that the royal Prince was still-born or so delicate that he was unlikely to survive, in her exhausted postnatal condition might well have been the fatal blow,' said Vince. 'So why not solve all her problems by substituting the lusty newborn baby of the willing Lady Reres or the Countess of Mar?'

'One thing seems certain, lad, that closed and devoted circle in the lying-in chamber had ample opportunity.'

'Do you think Mary knew?'

Faro shook his head. 'I think that the Queen was innocent of any deception and never believed otherwise than that the child placed in her arms on 19 June was the one she had just brought into the world. Listen to this letter she wrote many years later, from imprisonment at Tutbury in 1585, two years before her execution, "Without him I am and shall be of right as long as I live, his Queen and Sovereign, but he independently of me, can only be Lord Darnley or Earl of Lennox, that being all he can be through his father." '

'Sad and pathetic, isn't it, that her love and longing remained constant for the son she had not seen since infancy. He was ten months old when she abdicated in his favour and lost him for ever after Darnley's murder at Kirk o'Fields and her disastrous marriage to the Earl of Bothwell.'

'But didn't he plead his mother's cause with Queen Elizabeth,' said Vince, 'try to get her released from that long and terrible imprisonment?'

'No. Not once did he voice even the mildest protest. In fact, he made it so abundantly plain that he was hell-bent on securing the Crown for himself that even Queen Elizabeth was shocked by his eagerness to sell his own mother. "That false Scotch urchin!" she called him. "What can be expected from the double dealing of such an urchin as this?"'

'Since Elizabeth wasn't noted for her kind and gentle nature, then James must have been a monster, if not in outward shape then certainly in mind and heart.'

'Yes, Vince. But all the evidence points out that only substitution could decently explain his complete indifference to his mother's fate.'

'I agree. That picture of heartless betrayal is only less terrible if in fact James knew that there was no blood tie between them.'

'There is evidence, albeit too superficial to convince judge and jury, in his appearance too. Even in youth he had a wizened old man's face. His tongue was over large for his mouth; his personal habits were disgusting and obscene even when he wasn't slobbering and fondling his effeminate favourites. He was untidy, dirty, and as he seldom if ever washed more than the tips of his fingers he smelled abominably.'

'There certainly isn't much likeness in the portraits to either of his tall and strikingly handsome "parents",' said Vince.

'His mother was one of the bravest women who have ever lived, right through her life to her death at Fotheringhay. But James's craven cowardice was a byword and the legendary charm of the Stuart monarchs was replaced in him by political cunning.'

'"The wisest fool in Christendom", wasn't that what he was called?'

'Aye, and with good reason.'

'I wonder when he learned the truth?' asked Vince.

'It might have proved to be a secret very hard to keep. And in large families skeletons have an unhappy way of falling out of the cupboard when least expected. At a guess I would say he learned the truth from his tutor George Buchanan, who was Mary's enemy.'

'And thereafter lived forever in mortal terror of denouncement,' said Vince. 'No wonder drawn swords and any violent movement terrified him.'

'Aye, knowing what he knew. But not knowing how many other people were privy to the secret – and Scotland's nobles had a long and notorious record of getting rid of their unwanted kings. Very, very few ever died in their beds.'

'And if James VI of Scotland and I of England was an impostor, then he had good reason to be on the alert for assassins lurking behind every dovecot and in every closet.'

'And if the coffin in the wall contained Mary's real son, then the discovery of that long lost secret has more significance than any other episode in Scottish history.'

'I can see that, Stepfather. The curtain-raiser to the long-drawn-out tragedy of two succeeding centuries, culminating in the tragedy of Culloden, the downfall of the Clans and the doomed Jacobite cause.'

'And more up to date, Vince, we could also add the present clearances of the Highlands.'

'If Mary had died childless, then the whole course of Scottish history might have been very different. No Stuarts, no Charles I and no Charles II ... '

'Whose illegitimate offspring conveniently founded many of the most noble families in the land.'

'A very different "Kingdom of Scotland".'

'Or just Scotia, the northernmost county of England.'

'No Hanoverians, and no Queen Victoria,' said Faro.

'Our dear Queen isn't the most popular monarch Scotland ever had, if truth be told. You hear a lot of discontent voiced in the howffs of Leith Walk.'

'Aye, and we have it on good authority at the Central Office that there's a lot of dissatisfaction in Parliament at the amount of time she spends at Balmoral.'

'Behind the respectable closed shutters of the New Town, there are a lot of old men whose fathers were "out" in the '45 Jacobite rebellion. Even in England the early years of her reign, long before you were born lad, were fraught with problems. As well as the far corners of Empire, there were rebellions much nearer home – in Ireland and Wales.' With a laugh, Faro added, 'Get your Grandmother Faro on to the subject, wars are her speciality. If women had been allowed in Parliament, she would have made a superb politician.'

'God forbid,' groaned Vince. 'One woman ruling over us is enough yet the newspapers give the impression that her subjects are all devoted and loyal to a man.'

'Aye, and those same loyal subjects once demanded that her beloved Prince Albert be put in the Tower of London as a spy. There have always been assassination attempts on her life.'

'And, as you well know, not even Balmoral is safe.'

Faro nodded. 'When she's travelling in Scotland, the police are constantly on the alert. Never made public, of course.'

'Fenians?'

'Aye, but not only Irishmen.'

'So I gather. There had always been troubles in Ireland, but it appears that her loyal dominions, like Canada, are having problems.'

'I heard it being discussed in Central Office. Some trouble with French-speaking people who don't want to be Canadians?'

'More than trouble, Stepfather, it's a full-scale rebellion.' Vince gave him a hard look and said slowly, 'Only last week, Colonel Wolseley set out with a brigade of staunch men and Iroquois Indians to quell a threatened uprising.'

'How very interesting. I must read it up sometime.'

'Stepfather, why do you never read the newspapers?' asked Vince gently.

'I rely on you – and my mother when she's here – to keep me in touch with any interesting items of news. I'm too busy everyday with my own crime reports, lad, to consider wars and rebellions as a source of pleasurable reading. Especially in summer when our police are responsible for the safety of members of the Government – and the Royal Family – passing through on their way to Balmoral.'

Vince smiled. 'I'd have thought the first requirement of a detective was to be knowledgeable about current affairs.'

Chided but unrepentant, Faro indicated a file of papers on his desk. 'That's tonight's work. At any given moment I have to be able to reel off for Superintendent Mackintosh the whereabouts of every suspected lawbreaker and revolutionary in Edinburgh and the Lothians – aye, and a few north and south too, who might decide to extend their activities. In the circumstances, I shall continue to devote my leisure hours – the few I have – to the world of crimes I don't have to solve . . . '

Vince looked at the line of leather-bound volumes on the shelf. 'Such as Mr Dickens'?'

Faro nodded enthusiastically. 'Exactly. And times past – Scott, Shakespeare – how the spirit soars – I assure you a very necessary escape when a man has done wrestling with today's dark and sordid deeds.'

'You are incorrigible,' said Vince, with a shake of his head.

'That's as may be, lad, but let's not digress. Let's get back to Queen Mary and the question mark poised over the discovery of that tiny coffin.'

'And why so many might have died to keep its secret,' said Vince.

'And where do these', said Faro, indicating the cameos on the table beside them, 'fit into the puzzle? Let's hope

Lieutenant Mace has found the answer by now. He promised to track down a missing page of the inventory of the Queen's jewels.'

'And you think these might be on it?'

'I'm almost certain they will be.'

'You suspect they are part of a cache of buried treasure, don't you?'

Faro shook his head. 'I'm not sure what I suspect until we can learn a bit more about the man who died on Castle Rock. I must talk to Sir James's valet, find out what he knows about the jacket. Then I must try to track down Femister's daughter.'

'If she's still alive.'

'True. At thirty-eight, we hope so, if she hasn't succumbed to cholera or childbirth. We know who she married and where Lord Penfold still lives, in a handsome town house in Heriot Row. That is where I go next. But what became of Dowie, I wonder?'

'It seems very unlikely that he's still alive considering his serious injuries thirty-odd years ago. It's even less likely that he could be our dead man, seeing that broken bones heal but also thicken and the body was remarkably unblemished, apart from that tattoo on his wrist.'

'A clover leaf – for good luck, I suppose.'

'Didn't bring him much, did it?' Faro was silent. A second later he shook his head and said excitedly, 'No, lad, not a four-leafed clover – a shamrock. That's what it was. An Irish shamrock.'

'Of course. Poor devil.' Vince paused and then asked, 'Where next, Stepfather?'

'Tomorrow I'm off to Piperlees, but first of all I have to look into the Central Office and see what reports the constables have collected, if any, on my drawing of the cameo. See if it fits any of the stolen property taken during the Clavers gang's robberies. And if it does, then we may have a clue to the one with my father's papers.'

'After more than thirty years, do you think . . . ?'

'No, I don't, lad. That would be the easy solution.' Faro

shook his head. 'I think it would also be a miracle, but we must make sure.'

'And then?'

'Off to the Castle to see Mace.'

'Dr Kellar has promised me a day off. Rose and Emily are longing to see the Castle. We'll meet you there, of course,' he added hastily. 'That will leave you free to make your own arrangements.'

'And you, of course, free to entertain the enchanting Miss Haston.'

'Why, Stepfather,' said Vince in mocking tones, 'what an absolutely splendid idea. It's so sad to think of that lovely creature bored and unhappy in her gloomy Castle when she could be enjoying the benefits of fresh air and gentle exercise.'

'And where are you hoping to find that in the centre of Edinburgh, might I ask?'

'Oh, there are lots of places,' said Vince vaguely. 'We might go down the coast to East Lothian. The girls would love the seaside. And sea air is so beneficial, brings a glow to their cheeks.'

'Your conniving, Vince lad, brings a glow to mine. You are certainly in the right profession to make a fortune out of gullible patients.'

Chapter Eight

A hired gig took Faro out to Piperlees, where a long wait at the front door and the shuttered windows confirmed his worst suspicions. At length a horseman appeared on the drive, with the unmistakable look of a stable-boy.

'Heard you as I was going by. What do you want?'

'Is Sir James at home?'

'No he isn't. There's no one at home at this time of year.' And with an air of amusement and condescension at such ignorance of the gentry's habits, he continued, 'Now, where else would Sir James be but away up to Deeside for the shooting?'

'They were here in the midst of a party only two days ago,' Faro said sharply, furious at this further setback.

The stable-lad shrugged. 'Well, they've gone now. No, I don't know when they'll be back exactly, 'cos I'm not in their confidence. It depends a lot on the weather. Could be next week, or next month.'

'Are the servants with him?'

'Aye, some of them. Sir James is a good employer,' and, indicating the shutters, 'has the house closed up so that the other servants can get away to their own homes for a wee holiday too. What was it you were wanting, anyway?' he added, his curiosity aroused by this questioning and the brown paper parcel under Faro's arm.

Faro decided against declaring himself. The presence of a detective inspector on the premises might be calculated to spread alarm and despondency, put the innocent and guilty alike on their guard. By the time the family returned, tales of the 'polis's visit' would have gathered momentum among the tenantry. Rumour and speculation would be rife and Sir James, a personal friend of the High Constable of Edinburgh, would not be pleased at hints that his public record and private life were less than impeccable.

'I was wondering what Sir James does with his discarded clothes?'

'So that's what you're after, guv'nor, from one of them charity organisations are you?' Amusement was now replaced by contempt as he scanned Faro from head to foot, no doubt assessing the origins of the caller's wardrobe. With a shrug, he added: 'We don't get none of them down the yard. Her Ladyship packs them off to the poor house in Edinburgh, I suppose.'

Faro cursed silently at the prospect of continuing his quest for the jacket's new owner, faced by such daunting odds.

'What if there was something special – some garment too good to give away?'

The stable-lad shook his head. 'Might give it to his valet. But I wouldn't be knowing for sure. I'm only concerned with the horses and their welfare.'

'Is the valet around at present?'

The lad guffawed. 'Come on, guv'nor, where would Sir James's valet be but on holiday with the master? Doesn't move a foot – or a boot, come to think of it, without Mr Peters.'

Thanking him for his help, Faro limped back to the gig. Further investigation was pointless. The only person who could help him, if not Sir James himself, would be the valet, Peters. And next week or next month would be too late. By then all that remained of the dead man on Castle Rock would have been distributed among the eager young medical students from Surgeons' Hall.

On the outskirts of Edinburgh, Faro decided to call on Lady Penfold before going to the Castle. Heriot Row was bathed in milky afternoon sunshine. The day was oppressively warm, the heavily burdened trees silent of bird-song.

As he climbed the steps he felt certain that again his luck would be out. This was the time of day when ladies in Edinburgh society took a nap before calling for afternoon tea. The door was opened by a uniformed maid.

'Is Lady Penfold at home? Detective Inspector Faro.'

The maid glanced at the card. 'I will see if her ladyship is receiving visitors.' A moment later she returned and, opening the door wider, ushered him into the morning room. 'If you will wait here, please.'

Faro took stock of his surroundings. The perfect proportions of the Georgian room, the furnishings, the velvet and satin, the silver and crystal. He looked at the roaring coal fire in the grate and thought of this further extravagance for a late August afternoon. How sparse and even poverty stricken was his home at Sheridan Place. A waft of violet perfume announced the approach of Lady Penfold.

His first thought was that he had been mistaken, that the woman before him was far too young to be the Griselda Femister in the parish register. His experience of the *grande toilette* was limited, but she appeared to be attired in the manner of one going to a ball. With her flounces of satin and lace, and rich jewels, she was almost as over adorned as the room itself.

'Do please sit down.' As he did so, conscious of her ladyship's searching glance and, remembering Sir James's stable-boy's contempt, he was acutely aware of his own rather shabby dress.

Lady Penfold smiled. 'I'm afraid his lordship is away from home. We have just newly returned from abroad, a short summer holiday for a family wedding. His lordship's niece married an Italian count.'

As she warmed her hands before the blaze, her smile became coquettish. 'Weddings are such fun and all the noble houses of Rome and Tuscany were present. I revelled in every moment.' And with a faint shudder, 'I am finding Edinburgh a trifle chilly by comparison. Everyone who matters, all one's friends and acquaintances are away to

Balmoral or to shoot with some Duke or Earl of something on his estate in the Highlands.'

Another sidelong glance. 'Edinburgh is very dull and boring in summer. Do you not find it so?'

Faro shook his head. 'I'm afraid, your ladyship, that criminals, robbers and villains are quite indifferent to the conditions of weather. They even find certain advantages in remaining in Edinburgh when wealthy houses are deserted by their owners. The work of the police increases rather than otherwise.'

'The police? You are a policeman?' She sounded shocked.

'A detective. I gave your maid my card.'

'I'm afraid I did not look at it carefully. The silly girl is new here and all she said was that there was a gentleman downstairs. I presumed you to be some acquaintance and I have been trying in vain to place you. We meet so many persons in our social round, you understand.'

'I do indeed, your ladyship.'

'And you are a policeman?' She repeated the words carefully, as if giving this information time to sink in.

'Detective Inspector Jeremy Faro, your ladyship.'

She beamed on him. 'I thought you couldn't be just a policeman.' Again the sidelong glance. 'You look much too distinguished. However, you are surely rather young to have such a responsible position. You must be very clever,' she sighed. And Faro, managing to keep his face expressionless, received a look that even the most unobservant of men could not mistake as anything but an overture to flirtation.

The door opened to admit the maid. 'You will stay and take tea with me?'

Faro thanked her and the ritual of tea pouring and plate passing began, accompanied in the maid's presence by some trivial conversation from Faro concerning the splendid view of Queen's Street Gardens from the windows and a particularly fine collection of volumes of Sir Walter Scott, which he was invited to examine.

'They are all signed, Sir Walter was a close friend of

my father-in-law.' And in answer to his eager question, 'No, I have not read any of them, I'm afraid, I find there are too many pages and too closely printed to hold my interest for long. Candidly, I prefer real people and real-life adventures. So much more exciting than can be dreamed up in novelettes.'

And before he could think of a reply, 'Almost every day, life offers us some unique opportunity of experiencing a new sensation, a thrilling adventure, if we keep our eyes open.'

She looked across at him and her eyes, he observed, were very open indeed. 'Don't you agree, Inspector?'

Faro replaced the delicate china cup on its saucer. 'I'm afraid I haven't given the matter a great deal of thought.'

She lowered her gaze thoughtfully. 'You should, you know, you really should. Opportunities must often come your way, more than to most men. Such a very exciting and interesting life.'

'It can also be very dull. All routine enquiries are not as pleasant as this one.' That cheered her up considerably and he continued, 'Perhaps I may be permitted to explain the purpose of my visit.'

'Of course, Inspector. But I have enjoyed meeting you and I hope we will meet again. His lordship . . . '

'You mistake me. It is your ladyship I wished to see.'

'You wanted to see me?' The eyelashes fluttered. 'How absolutely splendid.' And leaning forward, eyes narrowed so that the pupils grew large and black, her lips slightly parted, she whispered, 'But really, Inspector, my conscience is quite clear.' And then stretching out diamond braceleted wrists for his inspection, she laid her soft cool hands on his. 'I suppose all criminals tell you that. Am I to have handcuffs now – or shall we say, a little later?'

Managing to remove his hands with a gentle smile, he said, 'Nothing so dramatic, I assure you. I only wish to recreate a piece of old history.'

'How very boring, Inspector.' And with a sigh: 'But if you must, I am yours to command.'

'I understand that both your parents died when you were a child.'

'That is so. I never knew my mother. She died bringing me into the world. That is why I am childless.' She paused and then asked, 'Are you a married man?'

'I was. I am a widower.'

'A widower. How sad.' But her look, hopeful again, belied such sentiments. 'Recently?' When Faro nodded, she asked, 'May I ask what happened?'

'My late wife died in childbirth.'

'So you are childless too.'

'No. We had two daughters.'

'How fortunate. I, alas, have always been so afraid, indeed so repelled at the prospect of all that agony that I have been grateful, nay, fortunate even, that his lordship had a son and heir by his first marriage. The first Lady Penfold died of a fever while they were travelling in Italy. Tell me about your poor wife.'

Faro shook his head. 'There is little to tell.' He could not bear to uncover his grief and agony over losing poor Lizzie and their longed-for son. The girls had been too young to understand, but Vince had been inconsolable. Part of his dedication to the study of medicine came from his determination to specialise in this branch of medicine with all its superstitions and prejudices. Dr James Young Simpson's discovery of chloroform in 1840 had been frowned upon by those who believed that ever since Eve it was woman's duty to bring forth children in suffering. For her ninth child, Prince Leopold, Queen Victoria had eagerly seized upon the use of chloroform thereby bestowing respectability upon painless childbirth.

Determined to change the subject, Faro said, 'Tell me about your father. How well do you remember him?'

'Not a great deal, I'm afraid. Except that he used to carry me on his shoulders down to the harbour at Leith to watch the big ships sailing away.'

'So you don't remember his accident?'

'Accident?'

'Yes. When he was killed working on the masonry at Edinburgh Castle.'

'Working on what masonry, Inspector? I don't understand you.'

'A wall in the royal apartments. He and another labourer named Dowie were repairing it, in 1837, in preparation for the Queen's coronation visit in 1838. The scaffolding . . . '

Lady Penfold held up her hand. 'A moment, Inspector. I am quite bewildered by your remarks. You have been grossly misinformed, I'm afraid. My father – a common labourer – a workman?' Her laughter had a strangled sound and before he could reply, she continued gently, 'You have got your facts wrong, this workman person cannot possibly be my father. John Femister was an officer and a gentleman and he died in the Canton rebellion in 1843. On the wall behind you is a painting of him in full dress uniform, the year before his death.'

Faro regarded the painting solemnly. There was little or no resemblance to the dead man on Castle Rock. She was watching him closely and there was nothing to be gained by refuting her claim. He apologised.

'Who brought you up after your father died?'

'A great-aunt in Fife. My only relative, alas, and now dead – the year I was married.'

'Was she also a Femister – from Ireland, were they not?'

Lady Penfold laughed. 'Ireland? Whatever gave you that idea, Inspector? These Femisters were Scots through and through. Great-aunt was on my maternal side, of course.'

'Of course. One more question. Did your father by any chance have a brother, possibly older than himself?'

'My father was an orphan, Inspector.' Her easy, flirtatious manner had been replaced by a certain watchfulness and carefully-thought-out statements. Faro had interviewed too many criminals in his twenty years not to know when someone was lying. He was certain that Lady Penfold was most anxious to conceal the truth.

Could there be any other reason than the very obvious

one: that she was a fearful snob, determined to impress with her good connections? Had she built this fantasy about her father, complete with portrait, in order to establish herself as Lord Penfold's wife and when she married deliberately turned her back on her humble parentage? A heartless verdict, but, Faro knew from experience, not altogether rare in those who wished to rise in society from a poor working-class background.

There was nothing to be gained by prolonging the interview, but as he apologised for wasting her time and bade her goodday, she made a rapid return to coquetry. With a great fluttering of eyelashes, she begged him to stay and tell her all about his fascinating work in capturing criminals.

He shook his head, murmuring thin excuses. At length, sighing, realising she had lost a conquest, she rang the bell for the maid to show him out.

'It is my turn to be curious, Inspector. What is your reason for all these questions?'

'Oh, have I not told you?' Faro faced her squarely. 'A man was found dead on Castle Rock recently and we had reason to suspect that he might in fact be related to your late father, John Femister, and that his fall was no accident.'

'You mean this – Femister person – might have been deliberately murdered.'

'That is what we suspect.'

There was a moment's pause as she sought to recover, then with a deep breath, she drew herself up and said sternly, 'I can assure you, Inspector, there is absolutely no connection with this house.'

Faro had observed her reactions carefully. Her horrified whisper, her sudden change of colour, her hands clasped tightly together, all were the confirmation he needed that this was indeed John Femister's daughter. Even more to the point he suspected that she had some knowledge of the dead man. What that connection was remained to be revealed and he was fairly certain that Lady Penfold would give him no help whatever.

As they walked towards the door, she said, 'It is only idle

curiosity, Inspector, but where do the police bury murder victims who are unclaimed by relatives?'

'They become the property of the Medical College. For dissection by the students.'

Her voice as she said goodbye was curiously unsteady, all coquetry long since forgotten. As the door closed behind him Faro had the satisfaction of interpreting her look of terror and guilt. The fact that her dreams that night might be haunted by remorse, and the thought of her discomfort, afforded him considerable pleasure.

At the Central Office there were six very short reports awaiting him, collected from the properties robbed by Clavers and his gang. In each case, according to the constable who made the investigation, Faro's drawing of the Queen Mary cameo had been carefully scrutinised and, in every case, the robbed gentleman denied ever having seen it before.

Superintendent Mackintosh came in as Faro put down the last report.

'If that piece is genuine,' he said indicating the drawings sternly, 'and no one has claimed it, then the proper place for it is in the collection at Edinburgh Castle. See to it, will you, Faro. Oh, and before you go, you had better sign this certificate for the Fiscal.'

The document related to disposal of the remains of an unknown man found on the Castle Rock. All the usual procedures of investigation had been carried out, but no claimant had come forward.

'He definitely wasn't one of Clavers' gang either, Faro. I had my informant take a look at him.'

Faro reluctantly put his name under the presumed cause of death – 'By misadventure' – and handed the document back to the Superintendent.

There was little point in protesting. A jacket that might have been distributed to the dead man by any of Lady Piperlee's charitable organisations, and not necessarily first hand. It could have had several owners.

Lady Penfold had been his last hope, a woman too

proud to admit a common labourer as her father, who had invented a grandiose background suitable to her present position in society.

He handed the certificate back and the Superintendent gave an approving nod. 'Good. That's settled then. Case is now closed and we can get him tidied away. Thank God. No one will be sorry about that, I can tell you. Complaints already about keeping bodies around in this weather, a very unpleasant business. Very nasty indeed, Faro.' And his reproachful glance seemed to indicate that his Detective Inspector had been personally responsible for the inconvenience caused.

He was leaving the building when a constable hailed him. 'Message for you, Inspector.'

Marked 'Urgent' the note read, 'Have stumbled on something which you ought to know. Come at once. Highly confidential.' The last words were heavily under-lined and the signature was 'Arthur Mace'.

'When did this arrive?'

'An hour ago, maybe more. I didn't realise you were in the building.'

But Faro was already at the door stepping into a waiting carriage. As it climbed the steep High Street towards the Castle, he felt the stirrings of excitement.

With or without the corpse of the mystery man, with or without his superior's approval, the case for him could not yet be closed.

As long as he had a shred of evidence.

And his sixth sense told him that whatever Lady Penfold's denials, however unsatisfactory the interview had been, her manner had betrayed evidence that the dead man was either a relative of John Femister or somehow connected with him.

It was by following such frail uncertain threads that mysteries were solved and Detective Inspector Faro brought criminals to justice.

Chapter Nine

At the entrance to the royal apartments, a gentleman, swarthy of countenance with the proportions of a wrestler and a decidedly foreign appearance which belied his very English name, announced himself as Forster, Sir Eric's personal assistant.

'Mace? Not here. On duty.' And without offering another word, Mr Forster retreated into his small office and closing the door firmly indicated that all further communication was superfluous.

Faro shrugged. No doubt Sir Eric would be able to contact Mace. As he walked across the corridor he thought about Forster's clipped English. His appearance and carefully enunciated words, few as they were, suggested that this was not his native language. The other explanation was more feasible, that Mr Forster was a Highland gentleman and that his native tongue was the Gaelic.

Entering Sir Eric's apartments, he found himself in the midst of a party which, by the evidence of the table set with the remnants of a considerable feast, had been enjoyed by an entire turnout of his family.

Rose and Emily were fully absorbed by a set of toy soldiers and a fort. This activity, he guessed by their rapt attentions, held more interest than playing with dolls long neglected in their nursery. Rose was bookish and Emily good with her hands.

By one window, Sir Eric and his mother sat in deep conversation. The closeness of their heads and the faint flush on his mother's cheek, her downcast eyes and shy smile, her hair untouched by grey, created an illusion of youth regained and suggested to her son that Sir Eric might indeed be renewing his past overtures.

Faro was happy to remain in silent observation to enjoy this delicious spectacle. How extraordinary that he had never until this moment seen his mother as other men might, as a still desirable woman. And he was also aware, for the first time, that Sir Eric's exceptional good looks and distinguished presence might commend him to ladies of all ages.

He had certainly failed to use his much-vaunted sharp eyes, his powers of logic and deduction where his own family were concerned. Wouldn't it be extraordinary if Sir Eric, that faithful family friend of forty years, whom Faro had long regarded in the affectionate guise of a foster-uncle, should become his stepfather? What would young Vince think about that?

From the other window embrasure, not clearly visible from where he stood, a woman's soft but sensual laugh reached his ears. The guffaw that followed was one he recognised and, taking a step forward still unobserved, there was Vince with Lucille, she looking down into the quadrangle and he watching her, narrowly, intensely, with his heart in his eyes.

Romance was most decidedly in the air; the two couples, a vignette out of a light operetta, were much too involved with each other to notice his arrival. To come suddenly upon the scene would be to everyone's embarrassment.

There was only one thing to do. He stepped back outside, knocked loudly and threw open the door.

His daughters noticed him first and, laughing, greeted his arrival with shrieks of welcome. He had given the two couples time to compose themselves and noted with some amusement that they greeted this interruption with perceptibly less enthusiasm than did Rose and Emily. He fancied that upon the faces of both men he detected fleeting shadows of annoyance.

His mother, however, managed to resume her mantle of caring motherhood with commendable speed. Had her boy eaten? Was he hungry? He was looking tired. Was his ankle painful?

Such concern made him feel irritable and quite a bit older than Sir Eric, whose overtures had obviously been receiving some encouragement. The magic of romantic dalliance had brought a youthful sparkle to his eyes and a new lightness to his step as he walked across to welcome the newcomer.

Lucille had meanwhile made a rapid transformation into the role of her uncle's hostess. In a very short time she had Faro seated in the most comfortable armchair with a stool on which to rest his ankle. Her personal ministrations further included a cup of China tea and a scone, heavily buttered and overflowing with raspberry jam, which she proudly presented to him.

Made suddenly at home by such thoughtful gestures and enjoying this charming young woman's undivided attention, out of the corner of his eye Faro was amused to observe his stepson's reactions. Vince was watching them with the same mutinous expression that in boyhood had followed the forcible removal from his grasp of some desirable but forbidden object.

Regardless of the potential hazards of raspberry jam, Rose and Emily both attempted to sit close by and hug him, at the same time regaling him with stories of their day.

'Dear Miss Haston has been so kind –'

'And dear Vince.'

'We have been everywhere in the Castle.'

'And met some real soldiers, Papa.'

Listening to his two daughters, Faro saw across the room Sir Eric relating some amusing anecdote to Vince, who appeared to have regained his good humour. Near the window the two ladies had their heads close together consulting a magazine devoted to the latest Paris fashions.

Faro smiled to himself. In a short space of time, the two couples had reverted to being four very practical people, all suggestions of romance carefully swept away as if he had imagined that golden glow when he first entered the room.

Putting down his cup and plate as soon as possible without offending Lucille, who seemed infected with his mother's determination to fill him full of scones and cups of tea, he left his chair with some difficulty and approached Sir Eric, wondering how he could politely extract Vince to tell him of the visit to Lady Penfold and the surprising developments.

'So glad you came, lad,' said Sir Eric.

'I'm here to see Mace, sir. He sent a note to the Central Office, saying it was urgent.'

Sir Eric nodded absently. 'I was just saying to Vince how I bless you for being so good to my niece while I was away. An old man like me isn't much joy for her. Needs taking out of herself. Had a rough old time of it at home . . . '

As he spoke Faro tried to direct Vince's attention to Mace's note, but his facial contortions were ignored and Vince, with a murmured 'Excuse me', seized the opportunity to withdraw once more to Lucille's side. Faro watched him helplessly before turning again to Sir Eric, only to find he had lost the gist of the conversation. Sir Eric frowned in his niece's direction in the manner of one who would like to say more and then, with a shake of his head, lapsed into silence.

'How was Balmoral, sir?' asked Faro tactfully.

'Oh, excellent. Some quite excellent fishing,' and then with a rapid change of subject, 'Mace, was it, you were wanting? Excellent fellow, Mace. Damned efficient too, not like some of these young officers. Splendid background in history. More use to you than Forster. Did he have any useful information on Queen Mary?'

'He did indeed. He was looking for a missing part of an inventory and I gather he found something . . . '

'Capital, capital. Then that's all settled.'

'Not quite, sir. I haven't seen him yet.' And Faro explained that the enigmatic Forster had told him Mace was on duty.

'But he should be off by six o'clock,' said Sir Eric. 'It isn't long to wait and you must make yourself at home with us meantime. In fact, why not join Lucille and me for dinner in the Mess this evening?'

Hearing her name, Lucille drifted over with Vince at her heels. 'Please come. We would love to have you, wouldn't we, Uncle?'

'I have already invited him, niece.' Sir Eric's sharp rejoinder sounded to Faro's ears unnecessarily irritable. Was this charming, high-spirited visitor beginning to pall on the elderly bachelor with his set way of life? 'We're taking your dear mother, and Vince, of course.'

Again addressing Faro, he smiled. 'No ceremony, just the regular chaps and I expect young Mace will be there. Chance for you to find out what this message was all about.'

Mary Faro, that normally shy and retiring widow, was all excitement as she turned to her son. 'Miss Haston's maid is taking the girls back home to Mrs Brook and – and Sir Eric assures me that I don't need to dress for this occasion.'

'You look quite lovely as you are, my dear, doesn't she?' Sir Eric beamed on the company in general to give their assurance.

'Your costume is quite perfect, so elegant,' said Lucille. Her wholehearted agreement and smiling glance in her uncle's direction suggested that this was a romance that would meet with her approval.

As Rose and Emily were put into their cloaks for the exciting drive back to Sheridan Place in Sir Eric's handsome carriage, Lucille whispered, 'Don't look so anxious, Inspector,' completely misinterpreting Faro's brooding glance. 'Bet is most reliable. And she dotes on children.'

Faro smiled. Fondness of children was the last thing he would have suspected of the dour-faced, enigmatic maid.

The room seemed strangely empty after the girls had left. Faro sighed. He missed them and found himself wishing that they had either stayed at the Castle or that he had accompanied them home. He felt suddenly that a fifth person was an unnecessary and not altogether welcome addition to the foursome he had come upon. Absorbed in each other's company, they were now forced politely to include him in more general and less personal topics of conversation, while he tried in vain to angle his bemused stepson aside to discuss more urgent matters.

As they took their places at the table in the Mess, Faro was unable to see Mace from where he was sitting. If the information implied by the note had been urgent enough to require his immediate presence, he felt a little put out that Mace had not made any effort to contact him before dinner.

Again he was conscious of urgency, of passing time. In a few days Rose and Emily and his mother would have returned to Orkney. Did that account for this feeling of unease, of living on a stage set with something monstrous lurking in the wings, and waiting for a cue that never came?

Lucille sat next to Vince, but it was to himself that she gave her undivided attention and catching his stepson's eye he received many a sad, cold and reproachful glance.

His mother was in deep conversation with one of their table companions. The subject was her favourite: politics. He listened to her candid observations on what was wrong with the French, as characterised by Napoleon III and the Prussians and, in particular, the shocking behaviour of French Canadians, unwilling to accept the benefits offered by British imperialism.

Looking up he saw Sir Eric watching her with a curious expression, a mixture of pride and apprehension. Conscious of Faro's gaze, he turned, smiled and proffered his cigar case.

'Your mother is a most remarkable lady. Shall we adjourn for a smoke?' he whispered. 'I doubt whether we'll be missed, this discussion could go on all evening,' he added with a groan. 'I know old Boyd once he gets an interested audience, particularly a pretty woman.'

And as they took a dram together, Faro studied his companion with new interest. Could it be that his mother's 'remarkable' qualities were the secret of her attraction for Sir Eric? And for the first time he realised that such a marriage would have made good sense, since his host was much too intelligent to wish for a merely decorative adornment to his drawing room.

Misinterpreting his thoughtful look, Sir Eric asked, 'I've noticed you looking rather ill at ease, lad. Anything troubling you?'

Faro shook his head. 'Not really. Except that I was hoping to see Mace.'

'Mace? Of course. I'd forgotten. The reason for this very welcome visit.' He frowned. 'Come to think of it, I didn't notice him at dinner, did you?'

'No.'

'To tell the truth, it completely slipped my mind.' Sir Eric thought for a moment. 'His fellow officers are usually seated at the far end of the Mess and in such a crowd it's difficult to pick anyone out. But he should be back in the main barracks now if you care to go and search for him.'

'If you'll excuse me, sir.'

'Of course. You know the way.'

Faro walked across the now dark quadrangle, where a rather lopsided moon seemed to mock at mortals. Its jaunty angle annoyed him, like a picture hanging askew on a high wall that he longed to set straight. When it suddenly vanished behind a cloud he shook his fist at it. 'All right, old moon. You're safe enough now but don't let it happen again.'

Suddenly he laughed out loud at his own absurdity, chiding an untidy moon. How many glasses of claret had he drunk? After the first two his glass had been constantly replenished by attentive servants, and he must have consumed at least the better part of a bottle.

At the barracks he was told that Lieutenant Mace had come off duty before dinner.

'You've just missed him,' said the young officer, giving directions. 'Room 223. Down the corridor, turn right. No, he wasn't at dinner. Bit under the weather, I imagine,' he added with a grin. 'We had a birthday celebration for one of the lads last night.'

Following directions, Faro tapped on the door, waited and receiving no reply looked inside. The room had an air of general untidiness with a dress uniform spread out on the bed, as if waiting for its owner who was going to need it in a hurry when he came off duty.

His way back to the Mess led him past the royal apartments. He stopped outside. Perhaps that was where Mace expected to meet him. But the doors were locked, the corridor empty.

'Where on earth can Mace have got to?' he said, returning to Sir Eric.

Sir Eric shook his head. 'The most likely thing is that having missed you and not knowing that you were dining here he has gone down to Sheridan Place.'

'You are probably right.'

'In that case, he'll be back directly.' Seeing Faro's look of preoccupation, he said, 'All right, lad, if you're worried, take the carriage. Roberts came back while we were at dinner.'

'That's very good of you sir. Will you tell my mother and Vince, please? They'll understand, they're used to my sudden arrivals and departures.'

Mary Faro, who had been watching them, came over. 'What's wrong, son?' When Faro explained about missing the Lieutenant, she nodded. 'Then we'll come with you. It's getting late.'

Sir Eric looked over her shoulder to where Vince and Lucille had their heads together deep in conversation. 'Shame to break up the party, Mary my dear. It's early yet. Besides we see so little of you,' he added, his hand coming to rest tenderly on her shoulder.

She smiled up at him and seemed to have no objection to his air of possession. 'But you're coming to tea tomorrow, Eric, aren't you?'

So it was Eric and Mary now, thought Faro. Well, well.

'And it really is late for me. I go to bed with the birds in Orkney and rise with them in the mornings.' Suppressing a yawn in evidence, she added, 'There you are, see – maybe that was the wine. You must forgive me, Eric, I'm very sleepy, all of a sudden.'

She paused to glance approvingly in the direction of the young couple. 'I'll just go with Jeremy, leave Vince to make his own way home.'

Sir Eric sighed. 'If you must go, then I'll see you down to the carriage.'

But there was no concealing their departure. Vince drew himself reluctantly out of the circle of Lucille's magic web.

'How boring that you must go, Inspector,' she said, pouting prettily. 'We were having such a lovely party.' At the door her whisper and the warm glance that accompanied it were for Faro alone. 'We have had so little chance to talk together. I do hope we are going to meet again very soon.'

Handing Mary Faro into the carriage, Sir Eric bent down and kissed her cheek. 'Good night, my dear. Sleep well.'

'Good night, Eric.'

Far from giving continued evidence of weariness, Mary Faro prattled happily all the way back to Sheridan Place with quite as much energy as Miss Haston had shown on a previous occasion. At last, asked a question, her son failed to respond.

'I'm sorry, Mother – what was that?'

She sighed. 'Nothing important, dear. You're very silent tonight.'

'I thought you were very tired, Mother.'

'You're a silly boy sometimes, son, but you're my very own.' She kissed his cheek, and he put his arm around her and with her head resting against his shoulder, they arrived at the locked gates of Sheridan Place. Dismissing Roberts and the carriage, Faro took out his key while Mary Faro looked up at the drawing-room windows. 'I wonder why Mrs Brook hasn't closed the shutters. And the girls' bedroom too, the early sun wakes Rose. She's always been a light sleeper.'

A sickness erupted in the pit of Faro's stomach as he unlocked the door. He knew only too well the unmistakable aura of an empty house.

'Mrs Brook! Hello – we're back,' called Mrs Faro, slipping out of her cloak. 'Shall we ask her to make us a pot of tea?' she whispered.

'She's probably gone to bed,' said Faro carefully. And trying not to alarm his mother unnecessarily, he added, 'You go on upstairs. I'll be with you in a moment.'

'No. I'll come downstairs with you. I must make a cup of tea. I'm so thirsty, I'll never sleep.'

Mrs Brook's basement kitchen was empty of all but the ghostly shapes of furniture, the phantom smells of cooking. He tapped on her sitting-room door.

'Mrs Brook?'

'Where can she be?' asked Mrs Faro anxiously.

But Faro was already across the room, tapping on the door of Mrs Brook's bedroom. As he expected, there was no answer. Looking inside, the bed was neatly made, still with its crocheted daycover undisturbed.

In a curious way, he realised that the deserted room struck a familiar chord of approaching disaster, a feeling of dread that he had been unable to shake off since he had opened the door of Mace's empty room in the Castle barracks.

Mary Faro looked over his shoulder. 'She'd never go out and leave the girls in the house alone, surely. Would she?' And before he could utter any reassuring words, she cried out, 'The girls, oh, the girls, Jeremy!'

Leaning weakly against the table, Faro heard her swift footsteps echoing up the staircase.

A second later, her shrill scream rang through the house. 'Jeremy, Jeremy, come quickly.'

And even as he tried ineffectively to leap up the stairs, she screamed again.

'Rose, Emily. They're not here. They've gone!'

Chapter Ten

The girls' bed was empty. The sight made Faro sweat. Pristine, neat as it should never have been at this hour, it conjured up the same sinister vision as Mace's bed with its sprawled dress uniform. If he hadn't been so damned desperate to see the Lieutenant none of this would ever have happened.

Even as his horrified realisation checked up the dreaded facts – that his daughters, who had left the Castle three hours ago, had never returned home – his mother was crying.

'Oh, my precious bairns. Where are they? I knew it, I knew it in my bones – that maid.' And with the certainty of hindsight, 'I never liked the looks of her, sly, sleekit, she was. I knew we shouldn't have trusted them to her. Oh dear God, Jeremy. Something must have happened to them. An accident, like your poor dear father – that's what . . . ' she whispered and, a hand over her mouth, she leaned against the bedpost, moaning and looking ready to faint.

Faro caught her as she swayed and held her to his side. 'Calm yourself, dear, do be reasonable now. If there had been an accident, Sir Eric's coachman – or the maid – would have reported it when he came back to the Castle – while we were still there. Mother, please, listen to me. He brought us home here in the very same carriage, remember?'

Mrs Faro dabbed at her eyes, tried to regain her composure. 'Of course, son, of course, you must be right. And he would have seen them safely into the house here first, surely?'

Faro hoped so. Sheridan Place was a public thoroughfare

for vehicular traffic during the day. After ten thirty the gates were locked by the lodge keepers and each resident had to use his own key.

'Then why aren't they in their bed?' she demanded tearfully.

'I don't know, Mother, but I'm sure there must be a very simple explanation. Since Mrs Brook isn't here either, we can conclude that they are with her, safe and sound.'

'Safe and sound. Two little girls who've never in their whole lives been out at this time of night? They should have been in bed asleep two hours ago, Jeremy Faro.' Eyes flashing angrily, she added, 'Don't be so stupid. I'm not an idiot, you don't fool me with your simple explanations. I can see it in your face, too, you're sick with fear as I am.'

Then sobbing she threw her arms around him. 'Oh dear God, how I wish I'd come home with them. I knew I should never have let them out of my sight.'

'You mustn't blame yourself. Nothing could possibly have happened to them between the carriage and the house . . .'

'I know what's happened. One of your criminals has kidnapped them,' she said accusingly. 'That's what. Or one of those white slavers . . .'

'Mother, please don't be ridiculous. White slavers wouldn't be interested in girls quite as young as those two.' It wasn't true and he knew it. He only wished that his mother hadn't put into words the terrible suspicion that had already crossed his mind.

By way of consolation, he smiled wanly. 'You surely can't imagine slavers giving that dour, sour-faced maid a second glance?'

'She's a woman, isn't she?' was the caustic reply. 'And that's enough for some men. Anyway, maybe she's in the plot too. In with the kidnappers . . .'

'Listen . . .'

At that moment, they heard the most welcome sound in

the world. A key in the front door, and the next moment Mrs Brook let herself in.

Mrs Brook. Alone.

She looked up at them, their horrified faces staring down over the banisters. 'Good evening, Mrs Faro – Inspector sir . . .'

'Where are the children?' shouted Faro.

'With you, of course – aren't they?'

'Come upstairs, Mrs Brook.'

'What's the matter? Has something happened to them?'

'Where have you been, Mrs Brook?'

'Me, Inspector sir? To the Women's Guild concert.'

'Until eleven o'clock?'

Mrs Brook drew herself up stiffly. 'I went to visit friends afterwards for a bite of supper. This is Saturday, Inspector sir, my evening off,' she added reproachfully. 'Or had you forgotten?'

Faro had forgotten. At his side, clutching his arm, his mother began to whimper. 'The girls – they weren't with you?'

'No, Mrs Faro. How could they be? They were with you.' And in a voice touched with panic, she whispered, 'Tell me – has something happened?'

'We don't know. Please sit down, Mrs Brook. We have been at the Castle and we stayed to dinner, sent the girls home to be put to bed by Miss Haston's maid. They aren't in their bed. Or anywhere in the house.'

It was Mrs Brook's turn to stifle a cry of horror as she looked from one to the other. 'But Inspector sir, they wouldn't be able to get in unless you gave them your key. Oh dear, if only you had remembered that it was my evening off.'

'You're not to blame, Mrs Brook. I expect they have gone back to the Castle. That must be it – and we've missed them.'

Faro tried to sound calm, watching them helplessly, the tears welling in Mrs Brook's eyes, his mother quietly moaning, and knowing he was only minutes away from having to deal with two distraught and hysterical women.

He thought rapidly. If only he knew for sure whether the maid Bet was back at the Castle. She had not been in evidence when they returned to Sir Eric's apartment after dinner. But that was quite normal. A lady's maid would stay in her room unless – and until – summoned by her young mistress.

If she had not returned, he could only conclude that she had let Sir Eric's carriage leave them at the entrance to Sheridan Place, presuming Mrs Brook to be at home. When they couldn't get in, she would have tried to find an omnibus to take them to Lothian Road. A stranger in the district, could Rose and Emily have helped her, have known about such things? And what if the maid had no money with her?

With a sick feeling of disaster, he realised that if they had taken any kind of transport, then she and the girls would have been back at the Castle long before he and his mother left.

Even if they had had to walk all the way.

So where were they? Where were his two precious bairns, his little daughters that he had always sadly neglected, who played such minor roles in a life where his duties as a detective inspector came always first and foremost. So relentless at tracking down criminals, he was suddenly made vulnerable by the presence of two small girls; had crime come to roost on his own doorstep?

Would he ever see them again? His mother hadn't been too far out with her speculations about white slavers. Every day small girls vanished from the poor streets of Edinburgh and Leith. Not for anything as exotic as white slaving, but for the thriving business of child prostitution.

Although arrests were few and the guilty were ready to pay a great deal of money to keep such scandals from being made public, Faro was grimly aware of this particular method of child abuse. The prettier small girls were first stripped of their rags, bathed and fed, before being led naked to the bed of some elderly debauchee for 'initiation'. Those who were not virgins bypassed the handsome private houses in the New Town, and were sent direct to discreet gentlemen's clubs patronised by Edinburgh's wealthy decadents.

Oh dear God.

The two women before him, both in tears, were speculating on what might have happened, neither of them, thank God, with an inkling of what he knew of that other society where no corruption that money could buy was inaccessible.

Numbly he stood, put out consoling hands, heard himself uttering platitudes, wildly untrue, as the doors of nightmare closed around them, while the ginger kitten Rusty the girls so loved demanded affection and a warm lap and was surprised and indignant at being denied them.

'Listen . . . '

'Someone at the door . . . '

Two raced down the hall. Faro hobbled after them.

This time the newcomer was Vince.

Vince. Alone.

Even as Mrs Faro threw herself sobbing into his arms, Faro looked at Vince's stricken face.

'The girls?'

'They aren't here?' whispered Vince. 'I had hoped . . . ' He followed them into the drawing room. 'Ladies, would you please make a pot of tea – very strong.'

'Tell me what has happened . . .'

'They are alive and well, so stop worrying.'

'But . . . '

'Tea. Strong tea, first.'

As the door closed, Faro seized his arm, noticing how pale he was. 'Is it true – they're alive and unharmed – you've seen them?'

Vince took his arm, attempted to lead him to a chair. 'Calm yourself, don't you go to pieces like those two. Stepfather, for God's sake . . . '

'Then for God's sake – tell me . . . '

Vince shook his head. 'All I know is that Lucille's maid

– Betty or whoever she is – came back to the Castle just before I left. She was in a terrible state. They couldn't get into the house, Mrs Brook was out . . . '

'Yes, yes – I know all that.'

'Then listen, for God's sake. The maid was in a state, wringing her hands. Rose was the only one to show presence of mind. She thought she knew the road where the omnibuses were. She had never been on one herself, but she was game to try it . . . '

'My dear, enterprising Rose,' whispered Faro.

'They boarded the omnibus all right but one stop further on and the driver put them off. The woman had no money to pay the fares. And now they were lost, but Rose thought they were near the Meadows and a short cut might bring them out near the Castle. They began walking and a gentleman's carriage stopped and when they explained their predicament, the coachman offered to take them to the Castle. They thought this was a tremendous piece of luck . . . '

'Luck, God Almighty!' said Faro. 'You know what all this implies, don't you, Vince, picking up children at night . . . '

Vince held up his hand. 'I'm trying not to think of that, Stepfather. And I advise you not to either. The facts are bad enough without us being over imaginative. We need time . . . '

Faro sank down on to a chair, buried his face in his hands. 'Time. We might already be too late, Vince. Even now your two stepsisters, my wee bairns, may have been violated by some rich pervert whose sexual impulses require . . . '

'Stop it, Stepfather. Stop this, at once!' Vince banged his fist on the table. 'For God's sake, let's concentrate on what we know happened, not what we think might have happened.'

There was a pause before the detective's alert mind gained possession over the distraught father. 'What else did this woman say?' he asked heavily. 'And how did she know it was a gentleman's carriage?'

'Because although it was empty, it smelt of cigars and pomade. She was quite definite about that.'

'Was she now? By God, I could kill her. And I swear I will if anything has happened . . . '

'She was guiltless, Stepfather. Gibbering with terror, I can tell you. She said that if it hadn't been for the presence of mind of one of the girls looking out of the window and noticing in the moonlight that Arthur's Seat was on the wrong side if they were travelling towards the Castle . . . '

'That would almost certainly be Rose, my bright, observant lass,' said Faro, his voice broken, near to tears.

'The woman said she then tried to get the coachman to stop, but he pretended not to hear and whipped the horses on faster. She guessed that they were being taken somewhere against their will. She then showed great presence of mind. The carriage had to stop momentarily at the crossroads, to let another vehicle pass, and she pushed the girls out. She intended jumping down after them, when the carriage took off again at high speed and took her with it. It stopped at some big gates – no, she had no idea where. She tried to get out and when the coachman saw that the girls had gone, he struck her down and when she came to, she – where are you going?'

'I'm going to the Central Office, to have every constable alerted.'

'I've already done that, Stepfather. On my way here. I reported two small girls abducted, and a constable left immediately for the Castle to interview the maid.'

'You stay here – tell the womenfolk any story you like. I'll be back as soon as I have news.'

Cursing the limp that hampered him when he most needed speed, Faro hurried towards Newington Road, where he found a hackney carriage setting down passengers. Grumbling about the late hour, the driver was persuaded to take the Inspector to the Central Office.

And there, walking towards a waiting police carriage was the most welcome sight in his whole world. Two small girls in the custody of Sergeant Danny McQuinn.

Faro called out. A moment later, he had them gathered to his breast. And for those prayers answered, a peace passing all understanding reigned in his heart.

'Papa, Papa.' Speechless, tearful with joy, he held them in his arms. 'We've had such an adventure, Papa.'

Over their heads, he looked at McQuinn, grinning with delight. For once, if there had been room he would have included his old enemy in that grateful embrace.

'Thanks, Sergeant.'

McQuinn grinned. 'I was just about to escort these two young ladies back home. Constable McDonald found them wandering along the High Street. That elder lass of yours – Rose is it? – shows great enterprise. Told me some amazing story, mind you, about escaping from a carriage on the Meadows.'

In the police carriage on the way back to Sheridan Place, hugging them to his side as if he could never let them out of his sight again, he listened to the rest of Rose's story.

'It's true, Papa. It was a horrid carriage, all dark and enclosed and smelly – with the blinds down.'

'I didn't like it one bit and that horrid maid of Miss Haston's pushed us out and left us to find our own way back,' was Emily's indignant contribution. 'We were lost, Papa, and anyway we knew there was no one at home.'

'You couldn't have seen anything anyway, you were so busy crying, Em. Luckily the moon helped and I managed to guess from Arthur's Seat and the Castle where the High Street might be.'

'She made us keep walking, for hours and hours, Papa,' wailed Emily. 'And I was so tired. Look at my best shoes. They're ruined, Papa. And they were so pretty. Grandmama will be so cross,' she added with a tearful sniff.

'Never mind, my precious. You shall have a new pair, I promise.'

'As I was saying,' interrupted Rose sternly, 'when I recognised we were near the High Street, after that it was easy. We saw a constable and told him we were lost.'

'I told him that you were our Papa,' said Emily.

'He took us to that nice Sergeant who was just going to take us home in the police carriage. But oh Papa, we were so glad to see you,' whispered Rose, snuggling a little closer so that she could kiss his cheek.

'We were very frightened, Papa,' whispered Emily.

'No, we weren't, Em,' said her sister indignantly.

'What a fib. I saw you crying once.'

'Just when we were very lost, and just a little bit, Em. But it was an adventure, wasn't it, Papa?'

One, thought Faro, that he fervently hoped he – and they – would never experience again.

'Do you think the nasty coachman was going to hold us to ransom?'

'Not really, Rose. I think it was all a bit of a mistake.'

'Mistake, Papa? How?'

He didn't want them to have nightmares. 'He might have been a little deaf and just didn't realise that you wanted to get out.'

'Then why was he going the wrong way?'

'Maybe he got the maid's directions wrong.'

Rose regarded him severely. Her small face registered disappointment. 'You don't really think that, do you, Papa?'

He didn't. But at that moment, the carriage stopped outside Sheridan Place, and leaving them to the rapturous reception from the three eager anxious people awaiting their arrival, Faro told the driver to take him to the Castle.

'It's very late, Inspector.' It was indeed.

The Castle gates closed at eleven and midnight was striking. He must content himself with a scribbled note, 'All's well. Girls safe and sound at home.' Leaving this with the gatekeeper to be delivered to Sir Eric immediately, he ordered the police carriage to return him to Sheridan Place.

As he looked out of the window, the moon was bright

as day and he felt a strong desire to propitiate the pagan moon goddess. What would have been the answer to tonight's sinister happenings if there had been no moon by which his enterprising Rose could recognise Arthur's Seat and discover that they were prisoners in a sinister carriage taking them in the wrong direction, away from Sheridan Place?

He shivered, longing to reach home where the girls were now safely asleep and there was laughter, smiling faces and a certain feeling of celebration in the air. Celebration – or was it deliverance from evil?

Suddenly he realised that the disappearance of Rose and Emily had put out of his mind all thoughts about Lieutenant Mace's failure to appear regarding the urgent message. A message which had brought Faro to the Castle in the first place and thereby set in motion the nightmare events of the last few hours.

He slept late next morning and awoke to the sound of church bells ringing. Downstairs Mrs Brook told him that his mother had taken the girls to morning service, leaving strict instructions that he was not to be disturbed.

Inspector Faro and Dr Laurie were lapsed Presbyterians, their kirk-going limited to somewhat perfunctory family occasions. Normally Vince took the opportunity of discreetly sleeping off Saturday night's hangover and did not appear until Sunday luncheon.

Hopeful that he might be awake, Faro looked into his bedroom. There was no response to his whispered 'Vince?', so ignoring Mrs Brook's lavish breakfast for his digestion's sake, Faro made his way up to the Castle.

He was anxious to speak to Bet and be in time to talk to Arthur Mace as he came off church parade. From the maid he learned that Sir Eric and her mistress had gone to morning service at St Giles's Cathedral, but her first question was for Rose and Emily.

'If any harm had befallen them, I would never have forgiven myself, Inspector. Never.' Her distress was obvious and the passion of her words genuine, making Faro realise once again that one should not make hasty judgements based on appearances only. Faces had their own reasons for presenting a dour expression to the world, but that did not mean that the hearts they hid were cold and uncaring.

'I'd like you to tell me what happened last night. First of all, why did you send Sir Eric's carriage away when you reached Sheridan Place?'

'Because the gates at the entrance weren't open, sir.'

That was true. After dusk they were locked and residents had to produce their own keys to gain admittance. As he listened to the maid's story, he realised it was almost word for word what Vince had related to him. At the end, she regarded his stern face apprehensively.

'You do believe me, do you not, sir?'

Some odd turns of phrase and her swarthy appearance had decided him even more than her faint accent that she was probably French.

When he said so, she smiled. 'From French-speaking Canada, sir. But I have been with Miss Haston's family since she was a little girl.'

And that fact put an end to any further doubts he might have had about the truth of her story. 'What about those big gates, where you managed to leave the carriage? Do you know how long it took you to reach them?'

'Ten minutes, maybe more. Half an hour? I have no means of being certain of the time.'

'You say that the coachman threw you out with some violence.'

'He struck me and, yes, I fell to the ground.'

'I trust you were not injured in any way.'

Again she shrugged. 'Not even bruised, sir. I fell on grass and I fainted only with fear, you understand.'

'Would you recognise those big gates again?'

She hesitated and then shook her head. 'It was moonlight, a road with a long wall. But I was so frightened and, as you know, Inspector, I've never been in Edinburgh before. I only know this area round the Castle here and, of course, Princes Street, where I go shopping with Miss Haston.'

'Have you any idea what was intended by this abduction?'

'Ab-duction – what is that, sir?'

'The attempt to kidnap the girls and yourself.'

She thought for a moment. 'It was not I they wanted, for sure. It must have been the little girls.' She looked at him steadily. 'Perhaps they hoped to hold them to ransom. Is that not the way with such kidnappers?'

'Only if they knew who they were, and I am by no means a rich man.'

At his words, Bet opened her mouth as if some thought had occurred to her, then she shook her head.

'Well?' said Faro.

She shrugged. 'It is nothing.'

'Allow me to be the judge of that, mademoiselle.'

'It is too silly, but – but it occurs to me that perhaps you were not the, er – target, is it? And that your little girls were never really in danger. That they were – somehow – only there by accident.'

Her slow speech as she sought for the right words made Faro unnecessarily impatient. 'What are you trying to tell me, mademoiselle?'

'Sir Eric – he is a rich man, yes?'

'Yes.'

'And he has influence with people in high places, yes?'

'He has.'

'And Miss Lucille is his niece – that is so?'

Faro agreed.

'I am only thinking that perhaps it was not myself and your little girls that the kidnappers wanted. You see, Inspector, Miss Lucille gave me her hooded cloak the day after we went to the shops on Princes Street.' She looked up at him. 'This was the first time I am wearing it.' She shrugged. 'Perhaps it is of no significance, but maybe this coachman made a mistake and took the maid for the mistress.'

A remote possibility but one worth bearing in mind. Faro asked, 'Tell me about this coachman. Would you recognise him again?'

The maid drew herself up stiffly. 'I do not look at such men, Inspector,' she said, a touch indignantly. 'All I can tell you is that he had a tall hat and was muffled up to the eyes, even though it was a warm night. As he never got down from his box, I do not know if he was short or tall, thin or fat.' She shivered at the memory. 'I was very frightened. Coming from the backwoods with wild beasts and wild men is one thing, but a respectable woman does not expect such behaviour in a civilised big city like Edinburgh and living in a titled gentleman's establishment.'

Faro hid a smile at her innocence, and thanked her for her presence of mind in engineering his daughters' escape from the carriage. Trusting she was none the worse for her adventure, he gratefully thrust a couple of guineas into her hand and went in search of Lieutenant Mace.

The corridor to Room 223 was deserted. He tapped on the door and, receiving no reply, opened it. He was not really surprised to find it empty again.

For some reason Mace was being very elusive, but what really disturbed Faro was that everything looked exactly as it had been last night, even to the dress uniform spread out awaiting the young officer's return. As neither it nor the bed had been disturbed, the obvious conclusion was that Mace had not slept in his room, nor had he returned there after dinner in the Mess.

Faro sat down on the only chair. He had to think this out. If Mace was missing, the connection with last night's events and the attempted kidnapping of his daughters on their way home from the Castle took on a very sinister aspect indeed.

The decision for the girls to go home with Bet in Sir Eric's carriage had been quite spontaneous. To believe otherwise was to take into account what appeared to be an elaborate string of coincidences, whereby the kidnappers had some connection with the Castle and that Miss Haston's maid and Sir Eric's coachman, Roberts, were in league with them.

And Faro found himself remembering how often of late he had felt sure that his house was being watched. He went quite cold at the thought of what such vigilance might imply.

And what of the missing Lieutenant?

Should he give credence to the maid's theory about her mistaken identity and, if the plot was to kidnap Lucille Haston, had Mace received some warning of what was to happen? In fact, had his information nothing to do with the Queen Mary jewel or the missing page of a sixteenth-century inventory? Dangerous information which threatened repercussions on Faro and all his family.

Chapter Eleven

As he entered Sir Eric's apartments, Lucille was removing her apple green satin bonnet, a perfect match for her gown. Her uncle, distinguished and resplendent in full Highland dress, handed Faro a glass. As he savioured the excellent Madeira, their first concern was for Rose and Emily.

Assured that the girls were well and quite unharmed by their ordeal, Sir Eric said. 'I took Roberts to task. He won't forget in a hurry that in future he waits with the carriage until his passengers are safely indoors. When I think of what could have happened to those dear children . . . '

'At least Bet didn't lose her head,' said Lucille proudly. 'I know you've never cared greatly for her, Uncle . . . '

Sir Eric shrugged. 'I was wrong. Worth her weight in gold,' and turning to Faro, 'good of you to come so promptly, lad. We were all desperately anxious, even after we received your message.'

'I really came to see Mace.'

'Mace?' Sir Eric frowned. 'I had quite forgotten. What was that about again?'

'I had a message from him. I believe it had something to do with this,' he said, taking the Queen Mary cameo out of his pocket.

Sir Eric and Lucille studied it carefully.

'Quite genuine, is it? Remarkably fine piece.'

Lucille took it and held it against her neck. 'To think that it is so old, and that the Queen of Scots probably wore it,' and closing her eyes ecstatically, she whispered, 'just like this, touching her bare flesh as it does mine, three hundred years ago.'

Sir Eric watched her with a tolerant smile as, suddenly shivering, she handed the jewel back to Faro. 'I'm not really sure that I would care to wear it, not after all that sad history.'

'You aren't likely to get the chance, m'dear,' laughed Sir Eric. 'I can't imagine the owner wanting to part with it. Must be worth a small fortune.' And to Faro, 'Who owns it, anyway?'

'We don't know.' He explained that it had been found on Castle Rock after the attempted break in and that, as it was unclaimed, Superintendent Mackintosh had decided it belonged with Queen Mary's jewels in the museum.

'Quite right, of course, once we have checked its authenticity. I'll get Forster to look into it. He should know – or Mace, even better. He's a very knowledgeable young man. I presume he's seen it.'

'He has.'

'I dare say he has found out something.'

'Do let us know. It's all very exciting,' said Lucille.

'What's wrong, Jeremy lad? You're looking very solemn.'

'I can't understand why he hasn't contacted me, sir.'

'Oh, I dare say he will.'

'But I went to his room and it didn't look as if his bed had been slept in.'

Sir Eric chortled. 'Come now. You obviously don't know army life, young lad, or what these chaps get up to. He would be off duty until tomorrow morning. Probably got a lady friend tucked away somewhere in Edinburgh and courting will have banished all other unimportant details from his mind.'

A clock struck and Sir Eric said. 'Good heavens, I had almost forgotten. You must excuse me, Jeremy lad, I have an engagement – a rather dreary Council meeting.'

As Jeremy prepared to depart also, Lucille sighed. 'I haven't any engagement for this afternoon, alas.'

'You may have the carriage, m'dear. Get Roberts to take you out somewhere and take your maid with you.'

Lucille smiled slyly. 'Perhaps Inspector Faro would escort me.'

'Good idea, if he's not too busy.'

'I am rather anxious to get back to the family. However . . . '

'Take the girl with you. Have the carriage. Your dear mother and the girls would enjoy a drive on an afternoon like this.'

'That's very kind of you, sir.'

'Not at all. Anything to keep this young lady entertained for a while.' At the door Sir Eric looked back. 'I will leave the pair of you to arrange things. Don't let her be a nuisance, Jeremy,' he warned.

'Beast,' shouted Lucille at the closed door.

On the way to Sheridan Place, he encouraged Lucille to talk of her life in Canada. Losing her parents when she was very young, he gathered that living with an elderly spinster Haston cousin and in a remote backwoods area had great disadvantages and severe restrictions. Little wonder that a young lady of spirit and restless ambition had been eager to escape.

'We only came across in May, you know. Uncle thought it advisable that we leave for a while as we lived in the Red River area, where all the trouble is brewing with the Metis.'

When Faro looked blank, she explained. 'Metis are half-breed Indians. They have a strong French and Roman Catholic culture and they resent being taken over by English-speaking, Protestant Canadians. Their leader is a very brave man called Louis Riel.'

She was silent for a moment and then continued. 'I didn't realise that I was going to be sent away to another backwoods. Orkney wasn't much better than Canada,' she said in disgust. 'And you can imagine, having heard so much of Edinburgh, I was so looking forward to coming to Uncle Eric for a while.' She sighed. 'Maybe things are always better looked forward to than when they actually happen.'

Faro smiled. 'That is one of the first valuable lessons in life, Miss Haston. Never expect too much, in fact, expect little and then one can never be disappointed, only pleasantly surprised.'

Lucille sighed.'You are so wise and I am such an idiot.'

Faro shook his head. 'No, not an idiot, just young.'

'Young.'

'Yes, young. And that is the one trouble time will cure.'

'You make it sound like an unpleasant illness.'

'And so it can seem sometimes. Growing up is not a condition of my own life that I would care to repeat.'

Lucille laughed. 'Oh Jeremy, you are so solemn. Why, I have been grown up for years and years.'

'Hardly.'

'It's true. I can scarcely remember what it was to be a child. Anyone living where I did, and with Cousin Haston, would not long be allowed the luxury of childhood, I can assure you.'

The carriage turned into the gates of Sheridan Place and Mrs Brook came to the door.

'I saw you from the upstairs window.' Seeing his startled expression, Mrs Brook beamed. 'No, nothing's wrong, Inspector sir. All is right as rain. When you didn't arrive back, we thought you had been delayed and seeing it's such a nice day and this is their last Sunday. Doctor Vince hired a gig and has taken them all to – where was it, now – Cramond, I think he talked about.'

A sublime day, Arthur's Seat shimmered, already crowded with small figures on its summit. Poor Vince would be furious when he learned that he has missed the opportunity of another visit from the delectable Miss Haston.

'You could probably catch up with them.'

'What a good idea.'

'Will you wait a moment, Inspector sir?' said Mrs Brook, darting back into the house.

Feeling benign, Faro turned to Lucille, 'Shall we got to Cramond? Would you like that?'

'I should like to go anywhere with you.'

Faro smiled, pretending not to notice the amorous glance, the gentle sigh that accompanied her whisper. He was giving directions to the driver, when Mrs Brook re-appeared breathlessly with a covered basket and a cloak over her arm.

'Those girls forgot the extra food I made for their picnic and Doctor Vince's bottle of wine. Oh, and here is Mrs Faro's cloak in case the sun goes in. If you don't mind . . . '

As the carriage trotted briskly towards Cramond, Faro told Lucille that this was their favourite place, how he had spent a considerable time canoeing with Vince during his student days. The tide was out and the island glittered across the causeway.

Lucille shaded her eyes. 'I wonder where they are?'

'Probably on the shelterd side. Shall we walk across?'

Leaving Lucille to give instructions to the driver to wait along the promenade among the other carriages lined up while their owners took the popular Sunday afternoon stroll across to the island, he took up his stick and led the way. Lucille insisting on carrying the picnic basket and wearing Mrs Faro's light cape thrown over her shoulders.

When they reached the other side, she exclaimed with delight at the sight of the canoes on the smooth water. 'What a divine place. But I don't see Vince and the others.'

'They are probably in the Dell. It's a rather secret place Lizzie and I discovered with Vince long ago. Sheltered and quiet, superb for a picnic. Yes, that's no doubt where they are.'

The Dell was empty. 'We must have missed them,' said Faro.

'Never mind,' said Lucille. 'We have the picnic, we might as well enjoy it. I'm hungry and I suspect you missed luncheon.'

That was true and Faro realised that he was indeed hungry. There were three boulders which he pointed out made a natural table and chairs. Spreading the contents of the basket, she said, 'What a divine spot. I can understand how you must have loved it here. And Vince must have been a great comfort to you after your wife died.'

'He adored his mother,' Faro replied, opening the wine.

'Tell me about her. I realised that you couldn't be his real father, you were too young. Does he always call you Stepfather?'

'Yes.'

'I would have thought Jeremy more appropriate.'

Faro shook his head. 'No, I like being Stepfather. It's like Father, I am the only one to be called that name by Vince.'

'Tell be about his mother.'

'There isn't much to tell.'

'Isn't there? She must have been considerably older than you.'

'Not really. She had Vince when she was sixteen. They were so close – more like brother and sister really.'

'You must miss her very much.'

When Faro didn't reply, she continued, 'Did she love you very much?'

'I expect she did.' He looked at her sombre face. 'What an odd question.'

'Why odd?'

'Because most people take it for granted that husbands and wives love each other.'

'I don't think it's always true, do you? And you are a strange man. You give so little away of your emotions.'

'That is because in my job emotions are best kept hidden.'

'Have you ever loved anyone since your wife died?'

Faro looked at her. To be honest or diplomatic. 'Well, yes, I have.'

'Then you would marry again?'

'I have no strong feelings on the subject.'

'Didn't you want to marry this other woman . . . '

'Do you mind if we don't talk about it, Lucille? It was all very recent and very painful.'

'She didn't want you? She didn't love you? How could she fail to love you?'

Faro shook his head violently, as if to shake away those terrible bitter memories of agony and guilt. Bad enough that they should still haunt his dreams and would, he suspected, for the rest of his life. He was certainly not prepared for – he did not even think he was capable of – a solemn discussion with this extraordinarily frank young woman about his past loves.

'Please – I've told you – I'm not going to discuss it.'

Seeing his expression, she put her hand on his arm. 'Forgive me, I've hurt you. I didn't mean to. Only I think things are best talked over.'

'Not for me. Not for me. And I don't think it's a very good idea for us to be on such personal terms.'

'Why not – what on earth is wrong in that . . . '

'Nothing's wrong, Lucille. Now let's talk about something else. There's a good girl,' he added, managing to sound to his own ears amazingly like Sir Eric. As the conversation slid, at his instigation, on to more impersonal topics, he began to relax. Although he kept a token lookout for his family, he was secretly pleased to have this unconventional and quite delightful companion all to himself for the afternoon.

Mrs Brook's box of candies was soon demolished, mostly by Lucille since Faro lacked a taste for 'sweeties'. However, the wine was heady on an empty stomach and he realised that he was suddenly tired, suffering from the effects of last night's terrifying ordeal.

As Lucille prattled on, back to her usual form, full of engaging trivialities and speculations, he found his attention wandering, hypnotised by the bright glare of the River Forth with its occasional canoes passing by, its white-sailed ships.

He blinked furiously, trying to stop his heavy eyelids closing. It was that delicious wine. He must have had several glasses more than Lucille and he was not a wine drinker, a good, solid, ale man. He thought yearningly of sleep. He might just close his eyes, Lucille would never notice.

Just for a few moments.

He dreamed that he was being kissed. The feeling was so real. Then he opened his eyes to find Lucille's face inches from his own.

He put his hand to his mouth and she smiled. 'I'm so glad you are clean shaven, I hate the fashion for beards. You have such nice lips, a firm strong mouth.'

Faro sat upright. This wasn't in the plan at all. He had no intention of making a fool of himself over Lucille Haston or encouraging her ardent but dangerous flirtation. 'What time is it?'

'It's early yet.'

'Is it?' And taking out his pocket watch, he struggled to his feet.

'What's the matter? We aren't going yet, surely?'

'Time and tide wait for no man, Lucille. And in this case, if we don't move sharpish the tide will be in and we'll have to stay here until tomorrow morning.'

'How wonderful – oh how romantic,' sighed Lucille, fluttering her eyelids.

Faro seized the basket, the glasses. 'Come along,' he said, offering his hand.

'No.' Reclining against the rock, Lucille shook her head obstinately and stared out across the Forth, a rebellious child again.

'What do you mean, no, Lucille?'

'I want to stay here.'

'We can't stay here. Don't you understand, once the causeway is covered the tide will cut us off until tomorrow morning.'

'Of course I understand. And I want to stay here – until tomorrow morning – with you, Jeremy. Just the two of us,' was the whispered reply.

Trying to misunderstand the implications of her remark,

he said lightly, 'Surely you don't want to stay here all night? I warn you, it gets very cold and uncomfortable.'

She looked at him directly. 'We have each other. Besides I noticed that there are cottages – someone will give us a room for the night.'

Faro looked at her. 'My dear girl, what are you suggesting?'

'Isn't it obvious? That we stay the night here.' And before Faro could do anything but continue to stare, she threw her arms around him, clinging, kissing his face. 'Uncle is sending me back to Orkney next week,' she sobbed. 'This is our last chance.'

'Our last chance for what?'

'Oh Jeremy darling, I love you. I love you so.'

'Nonsense, Lucille, you hardly know me at all. We have only met a couple of times.'

'What has that to do with it? I've loved you from when I first saw you. I know you love me and nothing else matters.'

'Lucille, dear child – even if I did love you as you imagine, lots of other things matter.'

'They don't, they don't – I love you and I will make you happy, I promise. And if we stay out all night . . . ' she stopped, looked at him.

'And if we stay out all night,' he finished slowly, 'what then, Lucille?'

'Then you will have to marry me, I suppose,' she said.

It sounded so absurd, so pathetically absurd and Faro knew that, even compromised, he would take the consequences. He could never share his exacting, dangerous life with this wordly-wise butterfly.

'Lucille, I don't love you.'

'I'll make you love me.'

'I'm far too old for you. You want a young man, full of hope in life, not a middle-aged widower with a growing family.'

'I love Rose and Emily – and Vince too. I'd make a good stepmother.'

Faro chuckled in spite of himself. He could just see

the kind of complications that might arise for Vince with a stepmother as attractive as this, and only a couple of years between them.

'What is so amusing about that? Besides many of my friends have married men a lot older than you. And I don't care for boys. Besides, I know about love.'

'I hope we all know about love, Lucille.'

'I don't mean in theory. I mean – I mean, well, I am not inexperienced where men are concerned. I have had a lover – one of the rebel leaders. That was why they made me come across to Orkney.' Seeing Faro's solemn expression, she laid her head against his shoulder. 'Oh, I shouldn't have told you that. It was very indiscreet of me.'

'And very honest too.'

'But it's made a difference. It's made you hate me now.'

'My dear girl. It hasn't made the slightest difference to my feelings for you. If I loved you and wanted to marry you, I assure you the fact that you've had a lover wouldn't matter a damn to me – or to any other decent man, I hope, who loved you.'

'Then why . . . '

'Look, Lucille, Sir Eric is one of my dearest friends. How would he feel if I stayed out all night with his niece, the girl he trusts me to look after?'

'We could make up a story. He would believe it. No one but us need ever know that we slept together. He likes you.'

'He would cease to like or respect me if I compromised you. He is a very honest, honourable man. And his greatest hope is that you will make a good marriage.'

'I don't want a good marriage. I only want you.'

'I doubt whether Sir Eric would be all that delighted to have a policeman in his family.'

'Even though he loves the policeman's mother?' Lucille giggled. 'I thought that would surprise you. And he has loved her for years and years. Oh Jeremy, we would be such a happy family.'

'No, Lucille. We wouldn't. I wouldn't be happy and

139

neither would you after the honeymoon was over. Detectives make very bad husbands. If you doubt that, ask Mrs Brook how often she makes meals and I don't appear, ask Vince how often arrangements are cancelled.'

As they left the Dell and began to walk towards the causeway, Faro heard the magic words, 'Papa, Papa.'

Rose and Emily were racing across the sands towards him, led by Vince and followed by his mother, a little breathless.

Explanations, exclamations of mutual surprise and delight followed. Vince had noticed Sir Eric's carriage and had come in search of them.

Faro hoped that Lucille's disappointment would not be obvious. But she rose to the occasion. As they hurried across the causeway, with the water creeping ever closer to their feet, Mrs Faro taking her son's arm with Vince and Lucille and the two girls racing ahead, Lucille's trilling laughter floated back to them.

'I'm so glad we found you in time, Jeremy. I don't know what would have happened if you'd missed the tide.'

'Nor do I, Mother dear.'

'That was a narrow escape you had.'

'It was indeed. The narrowest. And I was never so glad to see anyone,' he said, pecking her cheek gratefully.

Before boarding Sir Eric's carriage, Faro drew Vince aside. 'I must speak to you, then I will see Lucille home.'

Vince gave him a disagreeable look. 'Indeed. I rather hoped you were going to offer me that privilege.'

Faro felt compassion for the sullen, disappointed boy's face before him, conscious that he was helpless to avert the misery in store. Vince must go on with his hopeless infatuation for Lucille.

He must never know the truth. The truth that could only blight their happy bachelor existence. That it was the father Lucille Haston wanted, not the stepson.

With a sigh, Faro produced Mace's note. 'I would most willingly let you escort Miss Haston, but it so happens that I have to see Mace.'

As Vince read the note, Faro explained that Mace had failed to contact him. 'Incidentally, I have made some progress with the identity of our dead man – at last.'

Vince had dined with the Penfolds. He was immediately interested in Faro's abbreviated version of his visit, although Faro left out the flirtation.

'Come along, you two. Do stop gossiping.'

'What a dreadful woman. You must tell me more,' said Vince as the two parties made their farewells.

Faro, with a silent and subdued Lucille at his side, was driven back to the Castle, where Sir Eric was waiting for him, sitting at his desk, pen in hand. 'Been a bit of an accident, lad. Young Mace. Body's just been found. Cleaning an antique pistol, didn't realise it was loaded. Tragic business. I'm just writing to his parents.'

Faro realised that he was not surprised, that he had been expecting something like this. 'Have the police been notified? May I see the body.'

'If you wish, lad.' And looking round to see that Lucille was not in earshot, 'Half his face blown away. We had him moved to the barrack infirmary. And had the room cleaned up a bit.'

Faro groaned. And all the clues cleaned up too.

'Hell of a mess. You would wonder where all the blood came from.'

'You are quite sure that it was an accident?'

'Of course, lad. Forster heard the shot and rushed in, but it was too late. Called out medical man right away, but of course nothing could be done but sign the death certificate.'

'May I talk to Forster?'

'Of course.'

Faro could hardly reproach Sir Eric, but he did not enjoy the next half hour. This was the sickening side of detective work that he could well do without. He often thought his stomach was too delicate for viewing bodies that had died by violence, their own or someone else's. He found himself looking at the mutilated face, remembering that interview with Mace and wondering again why the young officer had failed to meet him at the Castle.

He found the silent, swarthy Forster waiting for him in the infirmary corridor.

'Sir Eric told me you were here.'

'I wish to see the museum room.' Forster led the way and opened the door.

Faro looked round quickly. Bloodstains had been washed away, a chair straightened. But there was nothing left in the way of evidence. And there was no place anyone could have hidden. 'Tell me exactly what happened.'

'Sitting in my study. Heard a shot from in here.'

'How did you know it was a shot?'

A faint smile touched Forster's face. 'People who live in military establishments do not make mistakes about guns and explosions.'

'You went immediately?'

'Yes. At first I thought the room empty. Then saw Mace's feet sticking out.' He shrugged. 'Quite dead.'

'There was no one else here. You are quite sure of that.'

Only one door. They would have had to meet me on the way out.'

'Could anyone have hidden anywhere?'

Forster gave him a penetrating glance. 'Before I went for the doctor and to tell Sir Eric, I locked the door behind me. I thought that was the proper thing to do.'

'It was indeed.'

'Thank you, Inspector.'

Faro looked at him quickly. Was he being sarcastic? There was no sign of anything but patience on the man's face.

'Will that be all you are wanting?'

'For the moment. Yes. You will need to sign a statement.'

'I have already done so. For Sir Eric and the police.'

As the man turned to leave, Faro said: 'One thing more, if you please. Are you quite satisfied that Mace's death was an accident?'

Forster thought for a moment before replying. 'Lieutenant Mace was an agreeable man. He did not make friends easily, or enemies either.'

'Can you think of anyone who might bear him a grudge?'

'No one.' There was no hesitation in his reply.

'He sent me a note. That he had found something important. I think it might have been concerning the inventory of Queen Mary's jewels. Do you know anything about that?'

'Only that he asked me for a missing page. I did not have it and told him it had disappeared when the items were being catalogued. It had been mislaid at the printers.'

'When was this and who were the printers?'

'A local firm who I am told were burnt down two years ago. All this happened before I came to work at the Castle.'

Dismissing Forster, Faro could not rid himself of the uneasy feeling that Mace's accident had been stage managed. For reason or reasons unknown someone had found his presence inconvenient.

If his suppositions were correct, then the exploding pistol was the work of the same hands that had pushed the dead man to his death on Castle Rock. He saw again that vision of a huge spread of wings above him and heard the rock crashing past him.

And all these dire events, he was certain, bore the mark of the same assassin.

Chapter Twelve

Vince looked at the note Mace had sent. 'Now we'll never know what it was.'

'If only I could have examined the body,' said Faro, 'that would have given some clues. But what can I do? I can hardly insist to Sir Eric that we have a full police investigation.'

'Death by misadventure is becoming somewhat commonplace, associated with these unfortunate jewels.'

'I have still some avenues left unexplored,' said Faro, taking out his father's notes. 'Tomorrow I shall try to interview Colonel Lazenby's widow. We've made enquiries and she still lives in the same house at Aberdale.'

The day was bleak, grey and the sunless peninsula echoed to the despairing cries of sea birds. Through the dismally unwashed windows of the hired gig, which had seen better days, Faro stared out along the twisting road, through a plantation of sea buckthorn, twisted and deformed into grotesque shapes by the harsh winds blowing across the Forth from the North Sea. Even on a sunny day, he suspected that the atmosphere of direst melancholy hinted at by those unhappy trees would persist.

The house, set well back from the road in comparative isolation, had a look of neglect, of continuing sorrow. The door was opened by an aged servant, whose suspicious expression suggested that there were few visitors.

'She doesn't receive callers.' And the door was about to be closed again. To say 'Detective Inspector' would further confuse and would be even less likely to gain him admission.

'Tell her, please, that I wish to talk to her about her late husband, the Colonel. My father knew him,' he said, with a complete disregard for the exact truth.

This statement did not have the softening effect he had hoped for. The servant leaned out of the door. 'Get away from here. Get away – at once.' Suddenly alert and looking over her shoulder into the dark shuttered interior, she said, 'And tell whoever sent you that Mrs Lazenby is not to be drawn on that subject. That subject was closed long ago.'

Faro was immediately alert. The maid's attitude was promising. It hinted at a mystery, and clues might be forthcoming.

'For God's sake, leave her alone,' the old servant now pleaded, almost tearfully. 'Let her stay in her daft world – she's safe from everybody there.'

'What is it, Wilson?' The voice was followed by a shadowy figure emerging from the gloom.

'Just a caller, madam. A traveller. Nothing important. Go you inside where it's warm.'

'A traveller did you say?'

'Aye. But he's away now.' As Wilson made to close the door, Faro caught sight of a pale face, long untidy white hair and a bedraggled gown. Wilson's attempt to close the door finally was impeded by Faro's walking stick.

'Good morning, madam. Have I the pleasure of addressing Mrs Lazenby?'

'You have, young man. And who are you?' And pushing the maid aside, she said sharply, 'Oh for goodness sake, Wilson, let me see him. Who are you? Who sent you?'

'I'm Detective Inspector Faro, Madam. My father, Constable Magnus Faro knew your late husband, the Colonel.'

'Theodore, Theodore,' she whispered and all suspicion vanished. 'Is there news of my darling at last?' An angry expletive from Wilson and Mrs Lazenby turned sharply. 'You may go, Wilson, I will take care of the gentleman. Come inside. I will be with you in a moment. Meanwhile, Wilson will prepare tea for us.'

145

Wilson bobbed a curtsy and ushered him into the dark hallway with a look of ferocious anger. 'Now you've done it, Mister Clever Detective,' she whispered. 'This was one of her rare times of being in her right mind. And now she'll be back again in that terrible darkness. All thanks to you. Damn you and damn all men.'

'What's that you're gossiping about, Wilson?' Mrs Lazenby had returned with a shawl covering her bedraggled bodice, in her hand some yellowed papers and a key.

'Just telling him I hope his feet are clean,' murmured Wilson.

'Quite correct. Quite correct.' And handing the key to the maid: 'Unlock the drawing-room door, if you please.'

'But madam – you can't . . . '

'Do as I say. We have a guest who knew the master.'

As he stood beside the frail old woman in the dark hall the smell of old flesh, long unwashed, filled him with faint disgust. From the opened door there floated out the disused air of many years, mixing with this miasma of human misery and tragedy. In this inappropriate setting he was even more conscious of bad odours than in the foul-smelling, rat and human infested warrens of Edinburgh's slums.

'And now the shutters, if you please.'

The room was flooded with light, revealing an expanse of ghostly sheeted furniture and ornaments, their outlines lost in the dust and tight cobwebbing of many years.

As if aware of the appalling picture of neglect before them, Mrs Lazenby gave a cry and tottered quickly towards what at first glance looked like a table, but seizing the sheet she revealed a grand piano. Coughing at the dust disturbed, she raised the lid.

'Theo's darling wedding gift to me. My beautiful piano. Listen to its lovely tone, sir. I play very well, he tells me.' She pressed out a few chords and hummed a tune which she tried in vain to find. With a sigh she put down the lid again.

'I seem to have forgotten it. I do play it very well.'

Suddenly she leaned against the piano and looked round, as if seeing the room for the first time. 'I was about to offer you a chair, Inspector. But I think we will be more comfortable upstairs.' With a shake of her head, she said, 'This used to be such a pretty, elegant room, Theo's favourite. It is a little large, of course, but so many parties, filled with people.'

And now it's filled with sad ghosts, thought Faro with a shiver, as he followed her up the handsome oak staircase. She opened a door.

'I trust you will not think it indelicate to be received in a bedroom. In my young day, ladies always received morning guests in the boudoir. But things have changed very much these days, not altogether for the better, I'm afraid.'

Faro looked round. If anything this room was more appalling than the ghostly drawing-room. Here was a temple of mourning and one that their dear Queen would have approved. What was worse, the room stank. And the next moment, he knew the reason why.

'This is the bed my beloved Theodore slept in. These are his sheets and his pillow. See the dent where his dear head rested. Nothing has been changed since the day he died, his nightgown and nightcap are there waiting for him. See. Over there his razors.' Pausing she opened a large wardrobe. 'And all his clothes as they were the morning he went out, went out never to return.' The sentence finished on a sob. Dabbing at her eyes, she continued, 'Do sit down, Inspector.'

He took the only chair, at her insistence, while she sat on the dressing table stool. What did she see in the mirror, he wondered? Not an old woman in a gown that had once been satin ruffled and now hung in filthy shreds and tatters, for, aware of his eyes and mistaking his expression, she smoothed one sleeve in a coquettish gesture.

'This was his favourite dress of mine. A little out of fashion, I fear, but I wear it for him, so that when he returns, he will know nothing has changed. Nothing.' She looked at Faro through the mirror. 'He is coming back soon? Is that what you have come to tell me, that his tour of duty has finished? Please tell me what I long to hear. I have waited so long.'

Faro was struck dumb. How could he remind this mad old woman that her Theodore had taken his own life, that her life with him had been a lie. That he had chosen death rather than return to her after his sordid involvement with the wife of a fellow officer had caused a regimental scandal.

As if interpreting his thoughts, she said, 'You must not believe what they tell you. There is no other woman, there never was anyone but me in Theodore's life. We live only for each other, live only for the days and nights we can be together. Soon he will have his dream – and mine – his son, our lovely baby son.' At that she began to weep. So sudden a change of mood caught Faro unprepared and he was helpless before this storm of grief.

The noise alerted the maid Wilson, who burst into the room. 'What have you done? I told you so, I told you so. Now I hope you're satisfied. Don't say I didn't warn you. Come on – out.'

'Wait a moment,' said Faro. 'I want to talk to your mistress. I'm sure she'll calm down.'

'Calm down.' The maid burst out laughing. 'Calm down. Her? You'd better go while you're safe, before she gets violent. When she remembers that this isn't nearly forty years ago and that her beloved Theo is dead and gone . . .' she sighed. 'A few more minutes, that's all it takes, then she'll be a raving madwoman.'

Faro looked at the sobbing prostrate figure now lying on the bed, as the maid continued, 'You wouldn't think she was very strong but she is. And violent too.' She rolled up her sleeves, showing deep scars, long healed. 'That was a knife she turned on me. I have other marks too, on my scalp. Everywhere. Come along, sir.'

At the front door, Faro asked, 'Why do you stay with her?'

The maid shrugged. 'Been with her since we were

both youngsters. She was only seventeen when she met the master. It was love right away and they got married before he returned to his regiment. They were married only two years when he died and she lost the wee lad. She was never sane after that, but I've stuck by her. I'll not let them put her away. She gave me a new life when I was going to be transported. I owe her that life and I'll stay with her till the day she dies.'

'Then why does she attack you?'

'She looks for the master. And when she can't find him, she thinks that I have done him in, in her poor confused mind.' The noise of sobbing had changed in intensity. The old woman was screaming now, beating her fists and her heels on the bed. 'Come quickly, Inspector, don't linger. If she doesn't see you before she opens her eyes, she'll have no idea that you were here. I'll tell her that it was another of her nightmares, soothe her with a drop of laudanum. With a bit of luck, she'll be right as rain in the morning, back again in her lost world, the poor love.'

'She has no idea what really happened to the Colonel?'

Wilson shook her head. 'Not now, not any more. She would never believe that he took his own life.' She looked at Faro. 'And it wouldn't surprise me if she was right at that. For I can tell you one thing, sure as God's in His heaven and Jesus Christ is His son, my master never committed suicide over a woman. That I'll never believe, no more than she does. He worshipped his young wife. After it happened, way back, she appealed, you know, tried to clear his name, but no one would listen.'

'This appeal – on what grounds?'

'Oh, she believed he was murdered and it was made to look like suicide. You see, he was left-handed, but the gun was in his right hand.'

'And did the police investigate this?'

'They didn't get a chance. It was a regimental matter, not a civilian thing, quickly hushed up. The police didn't bother themselves.'

'One of them did.'

'Oh, and who was that?'

'My father. He also died soon after the Colonel. In an accident.'

'My God. Is that true?'

Her words were lost in screams from the room above.

'I'll have to go to her. She may do herself a mischief. Listen to that.' The screams had turned into a tuneless chant.

'What's that? Singing?'

'Is that what you call it? This is where it all begins – the violence. I'll have to look sharp.'

Faro listened. 'That tune. That's the one she picked out on the piano.'

'That was the master's favourite. Can't remember its title, something about a red river. They used to sing it together.'

Those few chords mingled with the screams of Mrs Lazenby continued to echo dismally in Faro's head long after he thankfully boarded the waiting gig and headed for Edinburgh. An hour later with McQuinn and a police carriage, he set off for Piperlees.

The door was opened by the housekeeper. Sir James was not at home. At the sight of a uniformed policeman, and mention of a jacket that might have been stolen from Sir James, her attitude changed to one of cautious politeness.

'Sir James's valet, Mr Peters, might be able to help you.'

The house, built to look medieval, Faro recognised as being of fairly recent date. The lofty hall was not an unpleasant place to take a seat, surrounded by splendid portraits of Piperlees past and present, as well as their favourite racehorses and dogs.

Peters the valet was elderly. He descended the vast and heavily ornamented staircase cautiously, but to Faro's delight he recognised the jacket immediately.

'Yes, of course. I remember this garment very well. Sir James wore it about two years ago. A favourite of his, when it was the height of fashion. You will notice that the lapels

150

are narrower now, seats are broader, and – those buttons.'
Shaking his head, he added, 'How well I remember those
buttons and the trouble they caused, Inspector. You see,
Sir James lost one and we could never get a perfect match.
Well, the master being a stickler for perfection as you might
say, he refused to wear it ever again.'

'What happened to it after that?'

Peters frowned. 'I seem to remember that it hung in the
wardrobe for some considerable time, until he decided to
get rid of it.'

'Have you any idea who he might have given it to?'

Peters scratched his cheek thoughtfully. 'Now that's
a poser, Inspector.'

'Someone on the Castle staff, perhaps,' suggested Faro
helpfully.

Peters shook his head. 'Hardly, Inspector, more likely
one of the tenantry or some benevolent institution. We are
of a size, the master and myself,' he added ruefully, 'but I
am never allowed to inherit any of his grand clothes. He's
very strict about such things, bit of a hoarder. He would
get positively enraged if he happened to meet any of the
Castle staff wearing his discarded clothes.' He smiled
grimly, 'Especially his own valet, if you see what I mean.'

Faro sighed deeply. After this promising start, it looked
as if he had now reached yet another road that led to
nowhere.

'May I ask you how you came by it, Inspector?' asked
Peters with a nervous glance at the jacket.

'Of course. It was worn by a man who was killed in
an accident – and who had no other means of identification.'

'Dear, dear. Nothing to identify him. That was awkward.'

And Faro, on impulse, withdrew the cameo. 'Only this.
It was found beside him. Fell out of his pocket.'

'May I, sir? Very old, isn't it? Am I right in thinking
it's very valuable?'

'You don't happen to recognise it?'

'No. It isn't one of our treasures.' And as Peters handed

151

it back, Faro studied his face carefully. Unless the old valet was also a superb actor, he was speaking the truth. Noting the Inspector's doubtful expression, Peters added, 'You might ask Sir James when he gets back on Friday, Inspector – if you wish. However, you could take my word for it. I've served Sir James and his father before him for forty years. I think I can say I know every family trinket quite intimately.' And pointing to the cameo he said, 'That one I have never seen in this house before. I'm certain of it.'

Ushering Faro towards the door, and the waiting sergeant, he added, 'If you doubt my word, Inspector, you might have a word with Mrs Wheeler, the housekeeper. She's been at Piperlees for as long as I can remember and there isn't much that goes on in this family that she doesn't know about. She's a kindly soul.'

Peters rang the handbell and, as they awaited the housekeeper's arrival, Faro asked, 'Has Piperlees been troubled at all with this recent spate of burglaries in the neighbourhood?'

'No, thank goodness, we have not. We've been very lucky, or rather Sir James is a great stickler for bolts and bars on everything.' Looking at Faro, he smiled, 'Curious that you should mention those burglaries, Inspector, because it did just occur to me, that that piece, old and obviously valuable, might have come from one of the big houses.'

As the baize door opened, Peters introduced Mrs Wheeler and bid them goodday. 'Please let me know if I can be of further service to you, if you wish me to arrange a meeting for you with Sir James.'

Mrs Wheeler shook her head and confirmed Peters' statement that the brooch, as she called it, didn't belong to the Piperlee family. She showed even less knowledge on the subject than the valet. 'A pretty bauble, Inspector, and of course those jewels will be paste. They do these imitations very well these days, don't they? A body can hardly tell the genuine article any more.'

'What about this jacket, Mrs Wheeler? Have you seen

152

it before?' asked Faro, holding up the garment for her inspection.

'I should just think I have, Inspector.' And looking round to make sure that they were alone, she dropped her voice to a whisper, 'I know that the master dislikes meeting any of the staff wearing his discards, as you might say – and what an eagle eye he has for that sort of thing. However, when Mr Peters said it was to go to some charitable organisation I thought, well, charity begins at home. So I gave it to Jess at the bakery, for her old uncle.' She touched her head. 'He's not all there, poor man, but he's harmless, a good worker, too . . . '

'Works on the estate – out of doors?'

'Why yes. How did you know that, Inspector? When he was young he was a lumberjack and a gold miner, oh the tall stories he'd tell if he had the notion . . . '

But Faro was no longer listening, preoccupied with the vivid picture of a dead man, elderly with tanned arms and neck, and scratches on his arms.

Mrs Wheeler was shaking her head sadly. 'Such a lot of misfortunes, he'd had . . . '

'What was his name?' Faro interrupted.

'Name?' Mrs Wheeler seemed surprised by the question. 'Harry.'

'Harry what?'

'I don't know. We don't go in much for surnames among the estate folk, unless they're tenants.'

'What is his niece's name then?'

'Porter. Jess Porter.'

'And where does Mrs Porter live?'

'She isn't married – and she lives at the west lodge. Just go down the main drive, turn right then left, about five minutes away.'

Thanking her, Faro turned at the door and asked, 'One more question, Mrs Wheeler. Do you happen to know if Harry had a brother?'

'I think he had, older than him, but dead long ago.'

'Does he ever talk about him? About how he died, for instance?'

'He was killed – in an accident.'

'Do you happen to know where this accident took place?'

Mrs Wheeler's expression indicated that the conversation had taken a curious turn. 'In Edinburgh – I think it was up at the Castle.'

Again Faro thanked her, shaking her warmly by the hand. It all fitted perfectly and he had no further doubt that the dead man's name was Harry Femister, who would have been a young man in 1837 when his brother John died. He was so certain of his deductions that he sent McQuinn back to the police carriage with a message that they might have to take an extra passenger back to Edinburgh.

As he walked along the twisting, tree-lined path towards the west lodge he had a sense of jubilation. Here was the stroke of luck, the link he had hoped for. Found, he thought, with considerably less effort and legwork than he had bargained for. For once, fortune had smiled on him and soon he would have the mystery unravelled as well as the secret of the two Queen Mary cameos: whether they were part of a treasure hoard and worth another Queen's ransom.

A delicious aroma of baking bread, borne on the summer breeze, warned Faro that he had almost reached his destination.

'You can't miss the cottage, Inspector, it's one of the originals, a lot older than this house. Been here for two hundred years or more, thatched roof and all. Jess is the local baker,' Mrs Wheeler had explained, 'makes her bread in the same oven as her father and grandfathers before her. The Porters didn't go in much for progress.'

Chapter Thirteen

The bakery door was open.

'Miss Jess Porter?'

A plump and comely woman of about forty whose round-ed arms showed evidence of recent contact with flour came to the old wooden bench that served as a counter.

Faro's early training led him to realise how very impor-tant were those first thirty seconds of meeting and how many details, relatively unimportant at the time, were to prove of great significance afterwards. Even as he took in her pleasing appearance, he had observed that her eager greeting died on her lips. He was not the one she had expected. She was disappointed.

Once he had introduced himself, without further ques-tion she invited him into the large kitchen which served as bakehouse. Taking a cloth she wiped the table clear of flour.

'Take a seat, won't you. Would you like some refresh-ment? It's a warm day.'

As she bustled about the kitchen, Faro was aware that her eyes wandered constantly towards the window. He had only half her attention as she watched over his shoulder for that other caller so anxiously and imminently expected. Then, with a final despairing look, she took the seat opposite and spoke, as if suddenly aware of him for the first time.

'Inspector – did you say?'

'Yes, Miss Porter. We are making a few enquiries.'

'Enquiries?' And with a puzzled expression that betrayed nothing of fear or guilt, she set the jug of home-made lemonade beside him. 'Then I dare say it's thirsty work in this weather. Help yourself.'

Thanking her, Faro refilled his glass. 'I will, it's delicious.'

He was heartily glad of the cooling drink. Despite cooking smells calculated to stir even the most flagging appetite, the kitchen with its huge baking ovens was intolerably hot for a summer's day.

'What was it you wanted?' Jess asked.

'Mrs Wheeler told me that you have an uncle lives here with you.'

'He isn't at home just now. I can't tell you when he'll be back, either. Took himself off to Edinburgh a few days ago on a wee errand.' Her smile was cordial, unperturbed. Obviously if Uncle Harry had been contemplating a break in at the Castle, then she was in complete ignorance of such nefarious activities.

She paused and Faro prompted, 'What kind of an errand would that be?'

Jess laughed. 'Oh, don't ask me – I wouldn't be knowing that. Uncle Harry is a law to himself and he often takes himself off on little jaunts. Being a bachelor and so forth.' Then, conscious of Faro's unflinching gaze, she coloured slightly and said, 'Well, I might as well tell the truth, Inspector. You see, he's a wee bit – well, fey – simple, some folk hereabouts call it. Oh goodness, please don't mistake me, Inspector, he wouldn't harm a fly – not wicked with it, not that sort at all. It's just that he likes solitude, to commune with nature, he says, writes a wee bit of poetry and so forth.'

'But he tells you where he's going?'

'Sometimes, if he feels talkative.'

'And this time . . . '

'Oh yes, he had to see someone – at the Castle.'

Faro's sense of triumph was now suffused with the dismay and indignation he always felt in having to break the shocking and totally unexpected news to an anxious relative that the loved one they expected home was never to return. This part of police duty even after twenty years had never ceased to offend his natural humanity. He felt the sickness growing at the pit of his stomach and asked, 'Did he tell you why?'

She bit her lip, looked uncertain and then said, 'Well, I'm sure there was no harm in it. All rather silly, really – and romantic, but then Uncle is romantic. A long time ago – before I was born – his brother came across from Ireland because they were terribly poor and he expected to find the streets of Edinburgh lined with gold. He was disappointed, like a lot of other folk. Anyway, Uncle John . . . '

'John Femister, was that his name?'

'That's right. Well, he was strong and went into building work, got married to a nice Leith lass, my aunt Jean, and they had a bairn, a lass.'

A shadow darkened Jess Porter's face and Faro gave a silent hurrah at this confirmation of his deductions so far. It all fitted so perfectly.

'Then one day when they were doing repairs at Edinburgh Castle Uncle Harry's brother was killed in an accident. But Uncle Harry refused to believe it was an accident, some strange warning dream he'd had – I know you'll laugh, Inspector, but I told you he's fey. Anyway, he was sure it was part of some dark plot. Though why should anyone want to kill a poor Irishman working as a labourer? What could they possibly get from him? I can't think, can you?'

Faro shook his head obligingly and Jess added slowly, 'Unless there really was buried treasure. That's why Uncle Harry believes his brother was killed.'

A note of excitement crept into her voice. 'Their father was a school teacher and he taught them their sums and their letters. They wrote to each other, John trying to persuade Harry to leave home, but he felt honour bound to stay and help his father, dying of consumption he was. Two little sisters and no mother either. Then just before the accident, Uncle John wrote telling him that he must come without delay as he had found something that would make their fortune.'

'That's what he said – a fortune?'

'Oh yes. A fortune. The exact words. My goodness, I couldn't mistake that,' she laughed. 'I've had that letter read often enough to me through the years.' Hesitating, with an anxious glance, she continued, 'I'm sure it's all right telling you, being a policeman and so forth and I've no doubt he'll tell you all about it himself if you come when he's at home. He's always on about the buried treasure at Edinburgh Castle. Tells everyone and that's really how he's got the name of being a bit simple with folk around here. They don't believe a word of it – how there's a fortune hidden away in a hollow wall in the Castle for anyone that finds it.'

From his pocket Faro withdrew the Queen Mary cameo. 'Do you recognise this, by any chance?'

Jess laughed delightedly. 'I do indeed. That's part – the only part, I might add – of the treasure he's always going on about. Shows it to everyone who'll listen, "My only brother died for this and one day I'm going to find the rest of it." He's devoted his whole life to this quest, Inspector, he even went to the United States and Canada, worked as a lumberjack and a gold miner, to try to raise money . . . '

This was the second time he heard of Femister's work abroad and although he had only half-listened to Mrs Wheeler's account, he felt there was something else he should remember, some vital fact here that was in danger of being overlooked.

'What did you say?' He was aware of Jess Porter's anxiety as she pointed to the cameo.

'I said, Inspector, that my uncle never lets that out of his sight – or his possession. So how did you come by it?'

Solemnly he opened the parcel containing the jacket. At the sight of it, realisation slowly dawned, and she raised her hands to her mouth with a small scream. 'Oh – oh – something's happened to him . . . '

'I'm afraid so, miss.'

'Oh, how dreadful, poor Uncle. Is he – is he . . . '

'Yes, I'm afraid so.'

The tears welled from her eyes unchecked and suddenly helpless in the face of her grief, Faro took her hand. 'Oh poor dear Uncle. What was it?' she sobbed.

'He met with an accident in Edinburgh.'

'An accident? Him too? And he's dead? Dead,' she repeated. 'I can't believe it – I just can't believe it. Is he in the hospital?'

'No, miss. In the city mortuary. And I wonder, could you come back with me, just to identify him?' A convulsive shudder shook her and Faro stretched out a comforting arm. 'I know, miss, I know. It's not a nice thing to ask a young lady, but you seem to be his nearest relative.'

'I am that,' she sighed. 'His wife Jean was my mother's sister. I'm all he has since his other niece went up in the world. Her that married a title. I'll never forgive her, she could have done so much to help him. He wasn't asking for charity, just wanted a little money to help with his enquiries and he was willing to work for her, to earn something. Bitch that she was, she had him put from her door. "Don't let that mad old man come near my house again, or I'll get my husband to have him put away in the asylum."'

She began to sob again and Faro put his arm around her plump shoulders. 'Come, we have a carriage waiting down the drive, it'll take you into Edinburgh and bring you back home, of course. It won't take long,' he ended lamely.

'That's kind of you, Inspector, but I can't come this instant,' she said, with a glance towards the ovens. 'I have my batch of loaves to take out. That'll be another half-hour – and oh dear, there's my morning rolls to get in and by the time I get back . . . ' She made a helpless gesture. 'I'll never manage. And then . . . ' Again that glance towards the window.

'Are you expecting a visitor?' asked Faro gently.

'Well, not for me really. A man wanting to see Uncle urgently about some enquiry he had made.'

'Does that happen often?'

'Sometimes. He's always asking about history. I don't think he'll be coming now, but I'll leave a note on the door for him. If you'll wait till my baking's ready, please . . .'

In desperate need of breathing fresh cool air, Faro decided that sitting in this over-heated kitchen any longer was a frightful penance which even delicious home-made lemonade could not comfort. 'I'll wait for you down the drive.'

With his hand on the door, he turned: 'Those letters you mentioned – did your uncle keep them, by any chance?'

'Yes, he did, and they'll be in a big tin box he has hidden away in his bedroom.' She smiled sadly. 'I never let on that I knew about it, and I've never looked inside.' Her eyes filled with tears, and she took a handkerchief out of her pinafore. 'I don't suppose it will make any difference to him if I read them now, will it?'

'There might be something to help us with our enquiries. We'd be very grateful, especially as your uncle seemed certain that his brother's death wasn't an accident and if there is some evidence in those letters, then the police should know.'

'You're quite right, Inspector. He would have wanted that – oh poor Uncle,' she sobbed again. 'I'm sorry, Inspector, I just can't believe that all this is happening. He went out so bright and cheerful, just the way he always does – and now – this.' Drying her tears, she went to the table and with an air of determination floured the board and took up the huge baking bowl.

Faro watched her and asked, 'Did he have any friends in Edinburgh that you knew of?'

'A few drinking cronies and he used to visit an old friend who was in the hospital.'

'One thing more. Did your uncle ever mention a fellow he used to know – Dowie by name, dead long since, I imagine.'

'Peter Dowie, you mean.'

'The same.'

160

Jess Porter smiled sadly. 'He didn't die, Inspector. He's still alive – the one in the hospital.' She coloured and added, 'The East House.'

'The asylum, you mean.'

'Yes. Uncle just told folks it was the hospital. He didn't like to say asylum because folks round here thought he was a bit of a daftie, himself. And he knew it.'

'What about Dowie?'

'He's been there for years, he was a lot older than Uncle and he'd been crippled and gone the way old folks do sometimes, so they said, because of the accident long ago. Same one as killed poor Uncle John.'

So Femister was fey and simple and Dowie was senile. They must have made a pretty odd pair, thought Faro, as Jess continued, 'Uncle hasn't visited him for a while now. They told him at the hosp – asylum that he wasn't well enough to have visitors any more. That he'd turned violent. For a while Uncle went faithfully each week, but he gave up when they kept on turning him away.'

'Did you know him at all?'

She shook her head. 'When I was a wee lass, I went to the hospital with Uncle, but it frightened me, you know the way bairns are.' She smiled. 'But he seemed a gentle, quiet soul. It was a great shame, they were great mates, loved talking all about the past.'

Faro decided on an immediate visit to Dowie. Even in madness, there could be lucid flashes of the past which might yield useful information.

As he was leaving, with a reminder about the letters, she nodded. 'I'll just have a quick scan through.'

'The whole box would be a great help, miss, if you would.'

She smiled wanly. 'I don't suppose the dead have secrets any more, do they?'

He bit back the rejoinder, 'You would be surprised, miss, how many of them do. A look at our files in the Central Office would convince you.'

This was better, far better than he hoped. If it hadn't

seemed like an intrusion on her grief he would have offered to read the letters on the spot. Poor lass, she was very upset and taking it very well, trying hard to be normal.

As he limped back in the direction of the main drive, he discovered that his feelings of triumph and jubilation on having solved the dead man's identity had been overtaken by that strange sense of foreboding.

The closed-in path was overgrown and dim, the uneven ground made rapid progress difficult and when the bushes rustled at his side, he felt his scalp tingle with apprehension. This was so strong that several times he stopped and looked over his shoulder with his walking stick clutched as a ready weapon.

After the third time, he shook his head: I'm being fanciful, this won't do at all. But the shadowy arm of nightmare poised above the Castle Rock persisted, the moving shadow at the corner of his eye which swiftly melted into invisibility. The feeling of being followed by someone who was no fool, no newcomer to the business of tracking his quarry.

He was greatly relieved to emerge in the drive, where he found that McQuinn, at the housekeeper's invitation, had established himself in the kitchen and the handsome young Sergeant was surrounded by the usual bevy of twittering, admiring females.

As always, the sight annoyed Faro out of all proportion. McQuinn, who had so little to offer in the way of entertainment as a companion to his superior officer, beyond a taste for tuneless Irish jigs whistled uncomfortably shrilly at close quarters, was once again showing that he had hidden depths when it came to amusing the ladies.

'We're ready to move now, McQuinn,' he said with a brusqueness that quelled the maids and sent them scuttling away on their kitchen activities, with reproachful sniggers in his direction.

'Right, sir. Back to Edinburgh.' McQuinn, who could move very fast, could also on occasion act with such deliberate slowness that amounted almost to insolence. Heavy footed, reluctant to withdraw from his circle of admirers, he followed Faro on to the drive.

'Where are we off to now, sir? Carriage is down the drive.'

'I know that, McQuinn. I've found out who the dead man is – his niece is coming back with us to identify the body. We'll take the short cut – this way.'

'That was a piece of luck, sir,' said McQuinn prepared to be agreeable for once. He adjusted his long stride to his superior officer's stumbling gait, while Faro briefly supplied the details regarding Jess having recognised the jacket.

'The cottage is over there, where you see the smoke.'

'Looks like the lum's gone up,' said McQuinn.

'It's a bakery,' said Faro impatiently.

'Smells like burning thatch to me.'

Faro sniffed the air. McQuinn was right. 'Come on, hurry, man.'

Faro, using his stick to propel himself along, left the clearing just as McQuinn reached the cottage door. From every aperture smoke billowed out and flames shot from the chimney and the burning roof thatch. As he hobbled across with a growing sense of disaster, he saw McQuinn trying to open the door, his efforts encouraged by a small band of estate workers who had also raced towards the blaze.

When the door refused to move, McQuinn put his shoulder against it. Smoke billowed out and Faro limped after him.

'Don't come in here, sir. You stay clear, I'll bring the woman.'

Jess lay just behind the door and before McQuinn picked her up and carried her outside, Faro heard the crack of breaking wood.

'Keep away, sir,' yelled McQuinn.

Ominous sounds from above indicated that the roof was about to cave in. Through the smoke, Faro saw on the floor, near where Jess had fallen, a tin box. He seized it, winced with pain and threw the jacket over it. The roof collapsed with a thunderous roar as McQuinn laid Jess on the ground, her body hidden by the curious watchers. Faro pushed them aside.

'She's dead, sir,' said McQuinn, 'hit by a falling beam, by the look of it.'

Faro gazed helplessly down at her, the tin box in the jacket under his arm. Before them the cottage was already subsiding in a volley of small explosions and smoke, while Jess Porter's eyes were wide open, staring in disbelief as death had overtaken her.

One of the men pushed forward. 'We've warned her, haven't we?'

A woman took up the chant. 'Those ovens – far too hot, such heat she had for her baking.'

'With a thatched roof, we thought something like this would happen.'

'Mark my words, haven't I always said it . . . '

'Aye, a spark, that's all it would take.'

But was a spark all that had caused the inferno and why had it happened in such a short time? Turning his back on the curious watchers, Faro unwrapped the tin box. The lid was open and the papers in it, those letters dating from 1830 that he was hoping would shed so much light on Queen Mary's jewels, were charred, blackened.

Summoned by McQuinn's whistle, alerted by the smoke, the police who were waiting in their discreetly concealed carriage on the drive now raced across the clearing. Someone, smelling smoke and anticipating trouble, had had the foresight to bring a canvas stretcher and a blanket.

'Accident, would you say, sir?' said McQuinn.

Faro shook his head. 'It was no accident. The fire was deliberate.'

'The door was locked, sir.'

'Did she usually lock her door?' Faro asked a woman nearby.

'Never.'

'No, never.' The chorus was taken up. 'You could come by at any time of the night or day and Jess Porter's bakehouse door was always open.'

Faro walked carefully round the tiny garden. The glint of metal, in the sun beside a rose bush, was a key. The cottage had been set on fire, and Jess locked inside. When she died clutching her precious box she had been struggling to escape.

'I can't understand it at all, ye ken,' said one old man. 'Heavy thunder shower we had last night, thatch was wet through.'

'I ken that fine, Archie, I have a cottage just like this at east lodge.'

'I can't understand it. That thatch should never have gone on fire today.'

But it had and it had burned like a tinderbox, thought Faro, following the sad cortège across the clearing.

But the murderer wasn't to know that.

Faro cursed silently. This tragedy need never have happened. It was his own fault, he should have stayed, read the contents of the tin box while he waited for her.

He had no doubt that the mysterious visitor she had been expecting, who had wanted to see Harry Femister so urgently, had murdered them both. And the clue to the mystery would never now be solved for it lay in the contents of the tin box, the letters Henry and John Femister had written to each other, the charred and useless evidence that he now clutched beneath his arm.

Chapter Fourteen

Faro reached Sheridan Place anxious to accompany Vince on a visit to Peter Dowie, who, he was certain, was the last link in the chain of that day's extraordinary and tragic events. The authorities at East House Lunatic Asylum might react uneasily to Inspector Faro, but Doctor Laurie could produce impeccable reasons, not to mention powers of persuasion, for seeing a patient outside visiting hours.

Instead of finding his stepson alone, as he had hoped, he found the whole family assembled for yet another interminable mealtime. His own arrival had been eagerly awaited as the central figure in the ritual of suppertime.

'Do sit down, Jeremy. Didn't I tell you, girls, that Papa would be here in time?' said his mother.

As he hesitated, the door opened and Mrs Brook came in with the soup. He sat down reluctantly and around him, heads were obediently downcast, hands placed together in prayerful attitudes.

'Come along, Jeremy,' whispered his mother. They were waiting for him to say grace. Never had he felt less thankful, although he was hungry enough with only Jess's lemonade to sustain him. He seemed to have missed several meals that day.

'Amen. Amen.'

As soup spoons were wielded, Vince, seated opposite, obligingly passed the condiments.

'I hope you haven't an engagement this evening, lad,' Faro whispered.

'I was planning to take Lucille to a concert.'

'Can it not wait?'

'Indeed it cannot,' said Vince, outraged at such a suggestion. 'Why?' Then, glancing at his stepfather's solemn face, 'Trouble?'

Faro nodded. 'I'll tell you when we've finished.'

Catching his mother's reproachful glance, he gave his full attention to the soup.

'And what are you two whispering about?' she demanded.

Faro pretended deafness, while his more diplomatic stepson smiled and said winningly, 'Just passing the time of day, Grandmother.'

'Oh, is that the way of it?' demanded Mary Faro suspiciously. 'Well, whatever the pair of you are concocting, there's no need to eat your supper as if you haven't a minute left to live. You set a fine example to the children, I must say.'

Jeremy smiled wryly. His mother had the happy gift of arousing in a widower and a father approaching forty, the exact sense of wrong-doing he had suffered as a small boy. It was quite remarkable.

'Girls – Rose – Emily. There's no need to imitate your Papa, you don't want to have heartburn for the rest of your lives. Your complexions will be ruined and no nice young man will give you a second look.'

At this awful warning, the two girls ate with exaggerated slowness, gazing at dear Papa for approval. He gave them instead an embarrassed smile. Supper finally ended, they were loth to let him go. It seemed they didn't want to go back to Orkney next week.

'We want to stay here – with you – in lovely Edinburgh . . . '

'For ever and ever.'

If only their holiday had not coincided with his involvement in a new case. He was guiltily aware that he had spent precious little time with them, and that grudgingly and impatiently, his mind on more pressing matters. By next week he and Vince would be on their own again, the house's emptiness echoing to his remorse.

'Ready, Stepfather?'

'Yes, of course.'

Vince was already making their apologies, kissing and hugging the girls and their grandmother and promising that Papa would be back in time to tell them a story, with an impish glance in his stepfather's direction.

Faro gave him a cynical look. Oh, the stories that could be, and never would be, told.

Leaving the house, he asked, 'Can you get us into East House Lunatic Asylum?'

Vince chortled. 'Do you really think we're quite worthy of admission yet – we'll have to prove insanity . . . '

'We're going to visit Peter Dowie,' Faro interrupted sternly.

'Peter Dowie – the man who was so seriously injured in 1837? He's still alive?'

'He is – just, I fancy.'

'That's incredible, Stepfather. How did you come by this information?'

As they turned in the direction of Morningside, Faro told him of his discovery at Piperlees that the dead man's name was Harry Femister. Cutting short Vince's jubilant congratulations, he ended with Jess Porter's tragic death in the bakery fire.

'Dreadful – dreadful,' said Vince. 'Can you prove it was deliberate?'

'No. But I'm certain that it was.'

They walked in silence through the leafy suburbs. They were very near to the asylum when Vince said, 'When you consider our main list of characters, the discovery of that child's coffin has an alarming number of sudden deaths to its credit.' And enumerating on his fingers, 'Two deaths by drowning in 1830, two by falling scaffoldings in 1837 . . . '

'Let's not forget my father, lad.'

'My apologies. Plus one street accident and one suicide.'

'I'm not at all sure that Lazenby committed suicide.' And Faro gave a rapid account of his visit to the mad widow at Aberdale.

Vince whistled. 'How very odd – and she really believes that her husband was murdered?'

'Aye, and so does her maid. And what is more, I'm inclined to agree with them.'

'Which means that Lazenby's suicide might well have been a very useful method of dealing with an awkward situation?'

'Exactly. And the same goes for Mace.'

'Ah, so you think his death was murder?'

'Let's say I'm not happy with the label of firearms accident,' said Faro. 'It's all a mite too convenient, the body tidied away, the room cleaned up and no police investigation, if you please. This is a matter for the regiment.'

Vince thought for a moment. 'So today we have one death by climbing the inaccessible Castle Rock, one by a mysterious fire, one by exploding pistol. And if we add 'em all up including Lazenby's violent end . . . '

'Then we have nine potential murders.'

'You could well be right, Stepfather,' said Vince in awed tones. 'But why in God's name did these unfortunate people all have to die?'

'Because they were on to something so important that they couldn't be allowed to survive. Do you remember my father's last note?'

'The Egyptian-style curse, you mean?'

'No, lad, I don't. I'm as sceptical as he was about such things. "These devils will show no mercy" – human devils, Vince lad, definitely human.'

'About that fire, Stepfather, pity that the evidence was lost. You realise we have just about run out of clues.'

'Aye, a boxful of charred letters . . . '

'You brought them.'

'I did indeed. We have a man in the Central Office who's an expert in the particularly painstaking matter of deciphering charred letters.'

'What about this chap Dowie? You surely don't think a poor old mindless chap . . . '

'There might be some vital fact that he remembers.

And I'm rather relying on the cameos jolting his poor disordered mind with the clue we need.'

'You may well be right. It's exceedingly strange that the senile can be remarkably lucid about the past and decidedly vague about what happened yesterday. All their yesterdays become as one.' A moment later, Vince asked, 'One poser is – why didn't the mysterious "they" get rid of him too? They must have had ample opportunity.'

Faro sighed. 'Perhaps because he was hopelessly crippled, virtually a prisoner who could be cut off from the outside world. I imagine his visitors were very carefully scrutinised. Like Harry Femister, another harmless lunatic.'

'You're right, of course. Who would give credence to the fantasies of two daft old men about a buried treasure in Edinburgh Castle?'

'Aye, they were safe enough – until Harry Femister tried to prove it with his last desperate bid to storm Castle Rock.'

Vince shook his head. 'But why? That still doesn't make sense, Stepfather.'

Faro didn't answer. He was conscious that his pace had quickened as he remembered all the hours that had elapsed since his return from Piperlees. He had an overpowering sense of foreboding, that their visit to East House Asylum was already too late.

'I see that ankle is healing remarkably well,' said Vince as the gates came in sight.

Faro slowed down, suddenly aware that Vince's observation and the extra spurt of activity had not brought its usual painful reminder. He stared up at the grey stone building, which exuded a certain grim-faced respectability. There was an air of withdrawal and enforced seclusion about its narrow close-curtained windows with their iron bars.

As the bell pealed, Faro said, 'Say any prayers you might find appropriate, Vince, for mark my words, herein lies our last chance of success.'

The maid who opened the door had visage, colouring and a stern but remote expression in perfect keeping with her background, as if she had been specially chosen to blend with the institutional surroundings.

'Visiting's over for today, hours since. You're too late.'

Faro was wondering how any person could speak with so little facial movement when Vince stepped forward.

'I am Dr Beaumarcher Laurie, here to see a patient,' he handed her a card. As she read it somewhat reluctantly, he added, 'I am personal assistant to Dr Kellar who is no doubt known to you and I am to interview the patient . . .' He flipped open a pocketbook, frowned over a name, 'ah yes, Peter Dowie – in connection with Dr Kellar's research on mental problems. Dowie, we are given to understand, has been here for many years and has an interesting – a very interesting – case history.'

Faro listened to this pack of lies with extreme admiration as the maid, still doubtful, stared over her shoulder helplessly. Seeing none of the nursing staff, whom Faro hoped were off duty, and in mortal terror of offending someone in medical authority, she admitted them to the bleak and sterile hall.

Pausing only to consult a list and take a key from the appropriate numbered hook, she said, 'Night staff won't be here for an hour yet, but I expect it will be all right, you being a doctor.'

Vince nodded importantly and as they followed her along the deserted corridor the air of sterility was now overlaid with carbolic, in a losing battle to keep at bay less agreeable odours.

'Where are all the patients?' asked Vince.

'Locked up in their rooms, of course. Where else would they be? That's the rule, doors locked from eight at night till six in the morning.'

Their footsteps alerted the hearts of the imprisoned with new hopes of release, and their progress was followed by a tirade of screams and curses, sobs and pleas, animal howls, and furious banging on the locked doors as if a pack of wild animals was trying to escape.

As they climbed the stairs, the large window gave glimpses

of an Edinburgh suburb: its villas far below, with back gardens facing the asylum, were peaceful and domestic on this gentle summer evening. Children played on swings, a dog chased a cat up a tree barking fiercely, a couple sat at a table with glasses in their hands. Such scenes, such glimpses of normality played out against the screaming madness all around them, were an affront to the senses.

As the maid paused to unbolt yet another door, Vince pointed down to the scene below. 'Incredible, isn't it, that two such variations of humankind should inhabit so small an area.'

'I was thinking the very same thing.' It was appalling, the thought of those wild, tormented, mindless creatures, hopeless, locked away, unlikely ever to walk in a summer garden, feel the warmth of the sun or enjoy family life again.

'Is it quite necessary that they all have to be locked away?' Vince asked the maid.

'You know the rules. If we opened those doors, some of them would tear your throats out. They all believe that we are their enemies. Here it is. Room 49.' Pausing with the key in the lock, she turned to Vince. 'I presume you gentlemen are armed.' His non-committal nod was taken as agreement and she opened the door.

'You're lucky with this one. He's a cripple, out of his mind of course, but non-violent. He's had a fever recently, too. Weakened him considerably. You needn't expect much trouble.' She pointed to the candle. 'Light it, if you need. But be sure to blow it out before you leave. We don't want him setting fire to the room.'

Dowie's eyes were closed and he leaned back against the pillows. An old man with a mop head of tangled grey hair, a face pale and worn as the walls around him. At their entrance his eyes flickered open.

Vince leaned over him. 'I am Doctor Laurie.'

Dowie stared for a moment, trying to recognise them and then made the effort to sit up. 'Ah, a new doctor, eh? A new face and glory be to God a young one just for a change. Have you come like the good angels to set the prisoner free?'

'I've come to help you, if I can. And this gentleman too wants to help you. He is my stepfather.'

'Honoured to make your acquaintance, sirs.'

'We are friends of Harry Femister.'

Dowie smiled. 'My old mate, Harry – to be sure. And how is he – well, I trust? He has not been to see me for – for . . . ' He frowned. 'I cannot remember exactly. Time, hours, days, they are all the same to me – all the same – in this place.'

'You have known Harry for a long time.'

'Harry?'

'Yes, Harry Femister.'

Dowie shook his head. 'Long, long time. I forget when. But we were young lads. And I had two good strong legs on me then.'

Vince mouthed the words, 'John Femister, he's confused.'

Seizing the opportunity, Faro asked, 'The accident, what caused it?'

Dowie's mouth clamped shut and he shook his head violently, looking imploringly at Vince.

'What's the matter?'

'I'm not supposed to talk about it,' Dowie's voice sank to a whisper. 'I suppose you being a doctor . . . ' He leaned forward. 'If I don't forget, they told me, then they'll shut my mouth for good. They'll be after me again.' His eyes, bright now and suspicious, roamed past them searching the dusk-filled corners of the room. Suddenly he clutched Faro's arm, 'Don't let them get at me – for God's sake, keep them away from me.' Then aware of the strange faces, he cried out, 'Holy Mother of God, you're not the doctor. You're one of them – one of them.'

Vince came forward. 'Calm yourself, Mr Dowie. We mean only to help you. And you can trust my stepfather here, tell him all about it. He's a policeman, he'll see that no harm comes to you.'

173

'A policeman.' The old eyes regarded him with new respect. 'I've never had a visit from the polis before. Can you get me out of here – into the sunshine, for God's love – for pity's sake?'

'I'll do my best, if you can tell me everything you remember about the accident. Maybe then I can help.'

Dowie looked doubtful, turning his head from side to side, gnawing at his lower lip. 'I'm on your side, Mr Dowie, I've been fighting injustice all my life. As did my father, Constable Faro.'

The name obviously meant nothing to Dowie. He remained stubbornly silent. What pictures from the past were filtering through that poor demented mind, Faro wondered. He made a helpless gesture to Vince, who mouthed, 'Be patient.' At last Dowie seemed to come to a decision, nodded a few times and then said, 'We were working at Edinburgh Castle. Or at least that's what we had them believe. We were looking for King James, trying to find where they had hidden him away.'

'King James?'

'Aye, him that was Queen Mary's son and died – or was smothered – and holed up in the wall. An impostor it was took his place on the throne of Scotland – and England. An impostor who this new Queen is descended from, an impostor Queen who reigns over us now.'

'You have proof?'

'Aye, we could produce all the proof that was needed, if we found the body, it was all there.'

'All – you mean – a treasure trove,' said Vince.

The old man looked at him blankly. 'I don't get your meaning, sir.'

'The hidden jewels – where the cameo came from.'

'Oh, that.' Suddenly Dowie laughed and shook his head. 'There were two, a lad and a lass. John and I found them in the wee Prince's coffin. I gave mine to the constable who befriended me, for safe keeping. John's went to his young brother, as he would have wished.'

'What happened to the other jewels?' Vince persisted.

'There were no others, just those two cameos, lying on the Prince's crossed hands, one of his mammy, Queen Mary, the other of his daddy, Lord Darnley, proof positive that he was their bairn.'

'And that was all?' said Faro.

'It was enough, enough to bring the truth to light, the truth that has been hidden away all these hundreds of years. The body of Queen Mary's rightful successor, not only to Scotland but to England too, was all the treasure there was. If we made it public, got the people to believe us, we'd have them on our side, get the English out of our native land – usurpers, liars and cheats – they'd be the laughing stock of the whole world.' Abruptly he stopped, looking past them again, staring anxiously round the room.

'Your native land,' said Faro gently. 'Ireland?'

'Oh aye, Ireland too. But it's Canada is my home. I was taken there when I was ten, before all the troubles started.'

'Canada?' Vince and Faro exchanged glances. This was not what they expected to find. The predomination of Irish workmen who had met their deaths and what they now learned suggested a Fenian plot to discredit the monarchy. Dowie was whistling under his breath now, looking round frantically, a man who is conscious suddenly that he has said too much already.

'You were telling us about the accident.'

'The accident. Aye, they got two of the lads the first time. Before the Victorian Guelp as we called her, the bloody Queen of England came to the throne, there was a chance of revolution, of a republic. But in 1837 we knew it was now or never. The time was ripe. Prove that she and her whole line were impostors. Produce the corpse of the ancestor from whom she claimed her descent.' He chuckled. 'The succession was so shaky that the people would have seized any excuse with open arms. The scandal would have toppled the throne with a bang loud enough to be heard all over the world.'

'You almost succeeded,' said Faro. 'What went wrong?'

'Someone was on to us. They rigged up the scaffolding, made us walk on to it. John Femister and another Irishman, O'Hara, were killed. Both my legs were broken, my spine damaged. I've never walked again, but I'm strong, strong enough to survive. They thought I was useless and I suffered so much they expected me to die, otherwise they would have put paid to me on the spot. There was a policeman who knew what they were up to and he used some threat to expose them. Saved my life he did.'

He paused and looked across at Faro. 'He looked a lot like you, young man.'

Faro smiled. 'He was my father.'

Dowie nodded sadly. 'And a lot of good it did him trying to help us. They got him too, poor lad. Made it look like an accident . . . '

The door behind them flew open and a furious, red-faced matron filled the doorway. 'What is going on here. Visitors? Patients having their rest disturbed by intruders . . . '

Vince stood up and began to explain.

'I know Dr Kellar,' she said, 'but you will have to produce written proof from him before you disrupt my patients again. Now go – both of you – leave these premises at once.'

Vince's face was furious. He began to protest. 'This patient . . . '

'No,' whispered Faro, seizing his arm and nodding towards Dowie, 'don't make it worse for him.' And bending over Dowie, he inspected his wrists as he shook him by the hand. 'Good to meet you, sir.'

Dowie smiled sadly. 'And you, lad, remember me to your father.' And suddenly afraid at the approach of authority, he nodded towards the formidable matron breathing heavily at the door, outraged and impatient to have his visitors gone, and he grasped Faro's arm, 'Remember the Red River Valley men,' he said. 'Remember the Red River Valley.'

'At once, gentlemen.'

As the matron locked the door behind them, they heard Dowie whistling. Faro hesitated, for it was a tune he remembered, the one that mad Mrs Lazenby had played on the piano.

And he knew that he had solved two of the mysteries.

'Saw you looking at the shamrock on his wrist, same as Femister's,' said Vince as they walked down the drive. 'The good luck charm. So there was a connection.'

'There was indeed. But it isn't a shamrock.'

'No?'

'No, lad, and it's much more than a good luck charm, lad. I should have recognised that it wasn't an inexpertly tattooed shamrock at all. It was a maple leaf.'

'The symbol of Canada.'

'And I think that we'll find that this particular tattoo is also the badge of a dedicated band of French and Irish Canadians, dedicated to throwing off the yoke of British imperialism.'

'Of course, Lucille was telling me about troubles with the Metis, the half-breed Indians – the reason why she came to Scotland.' Vince whistled. 'So that's the reason for the murders, but who were the executioners?'

'Not were, lad, who *are* they? This is larger than individuals bearing grudges, we must set our sights on a relentless, well-disciplined political organisation.'

They had reached the main road where a horse-drawn omnibus bore the welcome sign, 'Newington'. As they took their seats and waited for other passengers, Vince said, 'I must confess that I'm a little disappointed. I was hoping for treasure trove and a reward for finding it.' When Faro laughed, he continued, 'We can only presume that the placing of the two cameos was a mark of respect for the Prince's unroyal burial. I wonder what became of those shadowy figures who placed the coffin in the hollow wall so long ago.'

'I imagine that everyone who knew was speedily eliminated, especially if they survived until King James was old enough to know and fear the truth. His years in Scotland were full of monstrous happenings, like the quite brutal murder of the Gowries . . . '

'You mean the Gowrie Conspiracy, when the Master of Gowrie and his young brother were assassinated by James's order, while he was a guest in their house?'

'That's just one incident – there are plenty more.'

'I wonder what kind of people they were, how they thought, Stepfather.'

'We can only judge their seeming barbarity by our own standards and I think we've had ample proof in this case that it hasn't gone out of fashion and we aren't any more civilised than our remote ancestors.'

Sheridan Place was a hive of activity, or so it seemed to one tired man who came home, envying his stepson's boundless energy. Too late decently to call upon Lucille that evening, Vince immediately rushed off to Rutherford's bar in earnest hopes of meeting up with his young friends Rob and Walter.

In the drawing room, Rose and Emily were seated at the writing desk, penning 'thank you' letters to Sir Eric and Lucille.

Mary Faro was reading the *Scotsman*. 'Have you heard what has happened to dear Colonel Wolseley?' she asked dramatically.

Bewildered for a moment, and preoccupied with his own forebodings, Faro stared at her, wondering for a moment whether this was yet another disaster at Edinburgh Castle for him to investigate.

'You really must read this, Jeremy dear, it's all about how Colonel Wolseley and his Iroquois Indians quelled a quite nasty rebellion.' Adjusting her spectacles, she observed her son's blank expression and laughed. 'To think that I was afraid to come to the mainland because of that silly man Napoleon. And there on the other side of the globe, these gallant soldiers were making that fearful journey into the wilderness, travelling by canoe, packed with ammunition and food, in unknown territory, down the rapids.'

With a sigh, she added, 'News takes such a long time

to get here. I have been following his Red River campaign most anxiously.'

'Remember the Red River people.'

Now Peter Dowie's parting words took on new significance.

'Think of it,' continued Mrs Faro, 'they arrived safely at Fort Garry, not a man lost, thank God, on the very day we landed in Leith and we haven't heard until we are about to leave . . . '

'You arrived here on 24 August,' interrupted Faro.

'Yes, son. Two days after your poor dear father's birthday . . . '

And the same day that Harry Femister's body was discovered at the base of Castle Rock. Faro stretched out his hand for the newspaper.

'May I, please, Mother?' He read rapidly of Wolseley's advance through heavy rain and deep mud on the fort, on the left bank of the Red River:

> When all were in position, our gallant troops stormed the fort. But to no avail. Their attack went unchallenged and a cautious investigation by brave scouts revealed that the place was deserted. The Metis leader, the traitor Louis Riel, had been forewarned and had fled, it is believed, to the United States of America.

The report ended with a glowing account:

> This was the first independent command of Colonel Wolseley, already being described as the best and ablest of soldiers. His campaign was most successful. It had accomplished its objective and not a life had been lost. The troops had benefited physically by their gruelling journey and had also gained invaluable experience in quelling future uprisings against the Queen's Empire.

Faro handed the newspaper back. Kissing his mother's cheek, he said, 'What would I do without you, dear?'

179

'The same as I do without you, my darling,' she said sadly. 'Miss you dreadfully.'

'Then I promise to come home to Orkney, very, very soon.'

'For Christmas, Papa,' said Emily.

'Please, dear Papa,' said Rose.

'Time you were both in bed.'

'We haven't finished our letters yet. Granny promised . . . '

Faro leaned over and regarded his daughters' efforts. Rose already wrote a neat copperplate while Emily battled with shaky capitals.

'I am ready to write the envelope. Will you do it for me, Papa?' she asked wistfully. 'Names and addresses are so hard to spell properly.'

'I'll help you with the spelling. No, you must write it yourself, or you'll never learn. Right? "Major General Sir Eric Haston-Lennard, Edinburgh Castle", that should find him.'

As the girls went upstairs with Mrs Brook, their father promising to read a very short story to them, Mary Faro picked up the envelopes and sighed. 'I shall miss Eric very much. He's such a dear, good friend.'

'Then invite him for Christmas too.'

Mrs Faro gave a little shriek. 'What? In my tiny house – what would the neighbours think?'

'I imagine they would think you were very lucky to have such a beau.'

Mary Faro blushed very prettily. 'Get along with you, Jeremy Faro, he isn't my beau.'

'But he would like to be? You know that perfectly well, Mother dear, and you're flattered by his attentions. I can see that.'

She sighed again. 'What it is to have a detective for a son – one hasn't a bit of privacy for one's emotions.'

He put his arm round her, hugging her. 'All these wasted years, the two of you. Why on earth didn't you marry him years ago?'

She looked up at him solemnly. 'I don't know, Jeremy.

I think I've always loved him, but something has always said, "No."'

'It's your silly snobbery – thinking yourself not good enough for him, that's all. It isn't too late to change your mind, you know.'

She shook her head obstinately. 'No. I had a bad dream just after your dear father died. Sir Eric was so good to us but I never, ever forgot it.'

'But Mother, dreams are nonsense. You can't throw away happiness for a dream.'

'I could for this dream. No – I'm not going to tell you any more, so don't ask me. Listen, that's Mrs Brook. Your daughters are ready for their story now, son.'

Next morning at the Central Office, Faro was in time to sign the papers identifying the dead man but not to halt the process of his being, as Superintendent Mackintosh delicately referred to it, 'tidied away'. And although Faro now knew the reason why Harry Femister had been on the Castle Rock that day, he could not change the clause 'Death by misadventure'. That must stand until such time as a murder charge could be brought, and first he had to catch his murderer.

'Well, Faro?' said the Superintendent. 'Get on with it. We're in for a busy day. Her Majesty left Balmoral yesterday. One of her whims to stay the night in Perth and proceed on another private visit to Peebles. She has expressly commanded that none of this is to be made public but we'll have to post extra constables as usual.'

'Are we expecting trouble?'

'No, but we'd better be prepared – just in case. There's a lot of isolated country *en route* where a Fenian could lurk. Don't suppose your services will be needed though,' he added sarcastically and turned his attention again to the papers on his desk in a gesture of dismissal.

In a room down the hall the charred contents of Harry Femister's tin box had been examined by the expert Sergeant Adams. Warned that they needed very careful

181

handling, since they would readily disintegrate, Faro soon discovered that what had survived were merely personal and not particularly literate or interesting letters exchanged between the two brothers.

He had almost completed his reading when Adams came in and set before him a crumpled piece of paper, which he smoothed out carefully.

'This came from the mortuary, Inspector. The dead woman had it clutched in her hand. I don't suppose it'll make much sense, but we have orders not to destroy anything till you have had a look at it.'

Faro picked up the paper. It was charred at the edge and it contained only the scrawled letters 'rich as'.

'Rich as – who?' Was this the last remaining clue to the Queen Mary jewels? Faro sat and looked at it for a long time, then he sharpened a pen and began idly to copy the letters in the hope that they might provide a clue. As he did so a picture sprang to mind. Of the last moments of a woman trying to fight her way out of a locked bakehouse, desperately trying to write a message. Another picture took its place. Of two small children laboriously writing at a table.

His hand trembled so much he could hardly pen the short note. At last he threw down the pen, engulfed by an icy sense of disaster which even the knowledge that he had solved the Edinburgh Castle mystery could not diminish.

'Found something interesting, Inspector?'

'Take this to Superintendent Mackintosh. Tell him where I've gone and that he's to come at once.'

Chapter Fifteen

At the Castle, Sir Eric was sitting at his desk, writing. He looked up, smiling. 'Jeremy, come in, lad. I've been expecting you. Do sit down.'

Faro remained standing. 'You know why I'm here.'

'Of course I do. From the moment I heard you'd found Dowie, I knew the rest was just a matter of course.' He gave him a shrewd glance. 'You're a clever chap, Jeremy, no doubt about that. Your dear mother must be proud of you.'

'Let's leave my dear mother out of this conversation, if you please.'

Sir Eric spread wide his hands. 'As you wish, dear boy. Anything you wish.' His manner was gentle, benign.

'Then first of all, tell me, who murdered Harry Femister? You know who Harry Femister is, I imagine.'

'I do indeed. A foolish old chap whose sympathies with the French Canadian rebels were well known. He climbed Castle Rock presumably with some idea of breaking into the royal apartments and finding that allegedly hollow wall on the very day Wolseley stormed Fort Garry.' He shook his head sadly. 'Only a madman would have tackled such a hazardous – and impossible – venture.'

'Who did you get to kill him – Forster?'

'Good Lord no. There was no need for anyone to kill him. The moment he set foot on the Rock, he was doomed. He had sealed his own death warrant.'

'Helped by one of your loyal servants, of course.'

Sir Eric shook his head. 'No, Jeremy, without any external help, you must believe me. His death was an accident, self-induced. He slipped and fell, a misadventure that could easily have happened to a young strong man half his age.' He sighed. 'However, it was just as well it happened that way. His attentions were becoming a bit of a nuisance, too persistent to dismiss as harmless eccentricity.'

'Was Mace's death also a fortunate accident?'

'I'd rather not go into that, if you don't mind, Jeremy,' said Sir Eric with a delicately expressive shudder. 'I'd have chosen a cleaner end then relying on his taste for antique pistols. He had come upon some evidence that we were not very keen to share with the world in general. And being a very moral chap, that was the only – rather messy – way to silence him.'

'You're admitting conniving at his death?'

'It was necessary. A soldier's duty to his Queen and country is to protect her at all times and Mace's information could have been disastrous to the safety of the realm.'

'What about all these other murders? All the people who died because they wanted to tell the truth – that the child's body in the wall here was that of Queen Mary's son, James, and that every monarch since has been descended from an impostor?'

'How romantic,' said Sir Eric mockingly.

'There's nothing romantic about eight murders.'

'Eight murders!' Sir Eric threw down his pen violently, an impatient gesture betraying the first emotion he had shown so far. 'Haven't you the least idea how many men – thousands, tens of thousands – I have ordered to certain death in the field in my years of army command – and you expect me to have feelings of guilt about a mere eight?'

'In the battlefield you were fighting against an enemy,' Faro reminded him.

'Is that so? Are not all men, eight or eighty thousand, composed of the same flesh and blood, capable of the same emotions, of feeling the same joy and pain? Besides,' he went on hurriedly, 'what do you think these men were but enemies of the Queen?'

'One of them happened to be my father.'

Sir Eric sighed. 'Magnus Faro was a fine fellow, one of the best who ever lived. I was sadder about Magnus than almost anyone I have ever known. Truly sorry, Jeremy.'

'Then I'm afraid you'll be a great deal sorrier when I do my duty to my Queen and country and arrest you as an accessory to murder.'

'You won't do that, Jeremy.'

'It is my intention, and who will stop me?'

'I will, lad,' said Sir Eric sadly. 'It is my intention that you are to be put under immediate restraint.'

Faro looked over his shoulder. Forster had entered with three other civilians. Of equal stature, they bore unmistakable signs of having served an apprenticeship in the wrestling ring. He braced himself. He was hopelessly outnumbered but he wouldn't go down without a fight. In a tight corner, he could give a good account of himself, for there were some very devious tricks he had learned in his time with the Edinburgh City Police calculated to throw even strong men off guard.

'Take him,' said Sir Eric tonelessly.

As they pinioned his arms to his sides, Faro said, 'Have you another accident in mind for me? I hope it's a convincing one this time.'

'You may rest assured on that score, Jeremy. We are very efficient in that department.'

'So I've observed. Tell me one thing, Sir Eric.'

'With pleasure, my boy.'

'You have been like a father to me, you supported my mother and I believe you have a certain fondness for her. You knew that I was in danger. How did you reconcile your conscience with giving orders that I was also to be disposed of, by an "accidental" fall of rock?'

Sir Eric regarded him steadily. 'You will keep forgetting that I am a soldier first and foremost, lad. Many times in my life I have had to obey orders, as you are doing now, because they were given by the highest in the land, Her Majesty the Queen herself. As you must have experienced

185

many times yourself, doing one's duty can be unpleasant, sometimes it can even wring a man's heart.'

He stood up. 'We are ready to leave now.'

'Where is Lucille?'

'Lucille should now be at sea on her way back to Orkney. When I suspected that you were on the right track and might arrive at any hour, full of accusations, I thought it best to terminate my niece's visit. Especially as the foolish girl seems to imagine she's in love with you.'

'Does she know anything of all this?'

'Of course not. She's a silly romantic girl.' He looked at Faro and that moment's compassion, more than any threats, chilled him to the heart. 'I'm sorry, I hope you don't reciprocate her feelings because I'm afraid you are unlikely ever to meet again.'

'Tell me, where did the plot to kidnap my two daughters fit into the plan? Was that just to scare me off too?'

Sir Eric shrugged. 'There never was any plot to kidnap your little girls, Jeremy. Their abduction that night was, I suspect, just what it appeared to be. Another attempted child abduction, common enough in the sordid annals of Edinburgh's underworld.'

He signalled to the four silent men. 'You know what to do.'

Faro was led by his captors, arms held firmly but unobtrusively, downstairs to a carriage waiting at the open door leading to the empty quadrangle. There was no point in crying out – nor any opportunity to do so – as he was bundled inside.

The window blinds had been drawn and one of the men tied his hands together behind his back while another blindfolded him. He cursed them roundly, realising that he was to be executed like a trussed fowl instead of being despatched, as he had always imagined, in a straight fight to the death.

The carriage moved off. They were travelling down the steep High Street. It was a road he had travelled often enough in his twenty years, strange that this was to be the very last time. Time, he thought, had almost ceased to exist for him. He had been denied even the condemned man's last requests, that he might say farewell to his mother, to Rose and Emily and to Vince. Especially Vince, dearer to him than any man alive, and very nearly his own son.

At last the carriage stopped. He was helped out and felt the warmth of summer sunshine on his face. Savouring that moment of finality, he took a deep breath before being led forward, warned of a step and propelled through a succession of stone corridors.

Were they going to put him in some miserable dungeon and leave him there to die? At least he was glad there was no resemblance to the creaking wooden floors of East House Asylum. They meant that he should have a less lingering end than poor Peter Dowie.

He realised that stone had given way to polished marble, for once his injured ankle, unused to such speed, slipped and only his jailers' support kept him from falling. Around him the echoes signified space, indoor space for there was no longer summer warmth or birdsong. He had the impression of a large room, the creaking of doors opening and closing, sounds of breathing, the clank of arms, as if the doors were guarded. Where in God's name had they taken him?

'Stand there.'

He did as he was told, wishing he could identify his place of execution. A moment later, the blindfold was removed. The large room was familiar. He was in the Palace of Holyroodhouse. He had been here before with the Edinburgh City Police during an attempted break in.

A tall man, grey haired, stood with his back to the window in the manner of one who does not wish to be recognised. A moment later, Sir Eric entered a little breathlessly, glanced at the document handed to him by the silent man and walked over to Faro.

'Got you here safely, eh, Jeremy.' He smiled. 'Sorry to keep you waiting.'

Sir Eric motioned towards the handsome desk across the

room, its only adornment an inkwell, sand and somewhat ironically a service revolver.

'Sit down, dear boy.' And walking across the room he put a paper in front of him. 'I'm afraid we will have to ask you to sign the Official Secrets Act, saying that you will not divulge anything that has been said between these walls or anything remotely connected with the recent disturbances in Red River . . . '

'And emphatically nothing regarding the possibility of a child's coffin being hidden in the walls of Edinburgh Castle,' boomed the other voice across the floor.

Faro began to read the document. 'You can believe us, it's all there as stated. Nothing else, nothing more.'

Faro looked up at Sir Eric. 'And what if I refuse?'

'I don't think you should, dear lad. Your freedom is in peril.'

'And what about my immortal soul, Sir Eric? Or maybe such matters are unimportant to you.'

Faro turned and addressed himself to the tall man, who seemed anxious to remain in the background despite his air of authority. 'I have done no wrong, sir. My only interest is and will continue to be to do my duty by my profession, by detecting crime and bringing criminals to justice. In such matters, I refuse to be compromised. And I'm not interested in being bought by anyone, not even the Queen herself.'

'Your attitude is commendable, but in the present circumstances inadvisable, very inadvisable,' said Sir Eric.

'You said there would be no difficulties, that he would sign. Get him to do so, dammit. We've wasted enough time,' said the other man.

Ignoring the interruption, Faro asked again, 'And if I refuse?'

Smiling beyond him, Sir Eric nodded, 'You had better ask Superintendent Mackintosh about that.'

Hampered by his bound hands, Faro swung round and came face to face with his superior officer, who had entered unobserved. Faro marvelled that the Superintendent, his one hope of survival, had come to his rescue without question and with remarkable speed. Did he have some plan for his escape?

'If you refuse, Faro, then I can tell you exactly what will happen,' said Mackintosh heavily. 'You will be dismissed from the Edinburgh City Police.'

There was a moment's silence, of disbelief, on Faro's part before he replied, 'So you are in this too. I might have guessed,' he added bitterly.

Mackintosh merely shook his head, looked at the other two men and made a helpless gesture.

'You convince him, Mackintosh,' said Sir Eric.

'Listen to me, Faro. Your loyalty to the Force does you proud. But if you don't do as they wish, I'm afraid, official sources will make it quite difficult for anyone to employ you – or your stepson, Dr Laurie, of whom Kellar is giving us such excellent reports. He has the makings of a brilliant career but your refusal to co-operate will destroy him too, especially as he has been concerned in your investigations.'

Faro saw all too plainly what his refusal meant. That the only place he could live in future would be in the ranks of the criminals themselves. What sort of life was that for him? But worse, much worse for Vince, at the beginning of his professional life, whose dream was to be Queen's Physician one day.

'If you are still in any doubt, take a look out of the window,' said Sir Eric. 'Oh, for heaven's sake, do untie him. Inspector Faro is a man of honour. He won't do anything desperate. You have my assurance on that.'

Untied, Faro left his chair, with one fleeting look at the service revolver, and the ardent wish he could prove Sir Eric wrong in the matter of chivalry. Moving stiffly to the window, he found that the room overlooked the private grounds of the Palace of Holyroodhouse.

And there was the last sight he expected on this earth: his mother, Vince, Rose and Emily walking together across the grass.

Brought no doubt just to make sure that I'd sign, he was about to remark bitterly, when he suddenly observed that all four of his family were wearing their very best clothes. They were all looking very happy and excited, especially Rose and Emily, who turned constantly towards a door directly below the window.

A moment later, he knew the reason why. A small plump woman, plain and middle-aged, in a purple satin gown, had emerged. A sudden breeze caught at the streamers on her widow's cap and as she half turned against it, the sunlight flashed on diamonds and emeralds, and touched the Gartar ribbon across her breast.

He watched his mother and the girls curtsy, Vince bow elegantly.

'If you need any further convincing, dear lad,' said Sir Eric at his side, 'HM is in it too.' And dipping the pen into the inkwell, 'Now, are you ready?'

The presence of his family outside removed any further hopes of escape and retaliation. Reluctantly he took up the document, added his signature, and as Sir Eric sanded it Faro indicated the revolver.

'Was that the alternative?'

'Think no more about it, dear lad. That is all behind us now.'

'And what if I had still refused to sign, after all these pressures put upon me and upon my family. What then?'

'A mere precaution – I've told you.'

'But if it had to be used,' Faro insisted.

Sir Eric shook his head. 'Then that would have lain very heavily upon my conscience. Disposing of you, and the sorrow it would have caused to one who is also dear to me.'

'But you would have done it.'

'Oh yes indeed. For I am as fiercely loyal to my duty to the Queen and all I hold dear as you are to dispensing justice.' He looked at him steadily and said quietly, 'If necessary I would have pulled the trigger myself. Come now, Superintendent, you will accompany us.'

And together, they marched with Faro across the room to the tall man who had listened with an expressionless face.

'You know Mr Gladstone, of course.' And handing the rolled document to the elder statesman, he said, 'And now, Prime Minister, shall we join the ladies?' And to Faro, 'You too, lad. Her Majesty has commanded that you and your family be presented.'